Matthew a
By P
Murder, deceit,
What was the final secret the ...... General took to his grave?

Part two of "The Trust"
The Trust is a series of four connected historical mysteries. Each one set in a different time period, each a stand-alone novel

Copyright © 2015 Pete Minall
Distributed by Smashwords
This is the second impression 2025
This book is licensed for your personal enjoyment only. This book may not be re-sold or given away to other people. If you would like to share this book with another person, please purchase an additional copy for each person you share it with.
If you're reading this book and did not purchase it, or it was not purchased for your use only, then you should return to Smashwords.com and purchase your own copy.
Thank you for respecting the hard work of this author.
Ebook formatting by www.ebooklaunch.com[1]

---

1. http://www.ebooklaunch.com

Table of Contents

Chapter One
Chapter Two
Chapter Three
Chapter Four
Chapter Five
Chapter Six
Chapter Seven
Chapter Eight
Chapter Nine
Chapter Ten
Chapter Eleven
Chapter Twelve
Chapter Thirteen
Chapter Fourteen
Dramatis Personae
About the Author
Authors Notes
Author's Acknowledgements
"The Trust"

Chapter One

August 1646

The two men looked out over the flat wide landscape, taking their time, studying the sky and the clouds as they rode in silence. Had anyone ever seen such a vast sky hanging over such remote beauty? The high white clouds scudding across the austere sky had a bleak beauty all of its own. Most people felt the eastern fens with its windswept, exposed, flattened land were both ugly and barren. To John and his companion Matthew it was home. Both men were constantly fascinated with how the grey, colourless skies and marshy lands could be suddenly transformed by the rushing of the clouds and shafts of sunlight appearing magically, bringing forth the colours of what was not only their home but the place where they did God's work. This day found them riding along the road, twisting its way between the waves of gently shifting reeds and grass, eddying and wafting in the gentle breezes, all bravely dipping their toes into the waters of the fens which edged the raised road. As the companions rode placidly and steadily on their journey they marvelled at the oneness of nature, the contemplative silence of the day only being broken by the sharp shriek of the odd bird disturbed by their imminent presence, all flapping wildly to gain height and safety from the approaching interlopers. Their destination was Kings Lynn, a town to which they had been summoned to do their duty. At least the Civil War, the war without an enemy, which often pitted friend against friend and brother against brother had all but died down, the army of Parliament had now all but won the conflict. This time of bitter conflict where Englishmen fought against and killed their fellow Englishmen was seemingly at an end. Matthew and John both hated what had happened to their country, especially as it had allowed Devilish works to propagate unchecked. Rumours had already begun to circulate that this may not be the end of hostilities as the New Model Army were said to be discontented with many of Parliament's actions. Matthew prayed this breach would not widen and that the rumours he had heard of insurrection would prove to be wrong. John and Matthew were both thankful that the threat of war was not raging around them here, as in some less fortunate parts of the Kingdom. One thing less for John and Matthew to contend with in their already stress filled lives.

This whole eastern area of the country was home to Oliver Cromwell who had been raising and training his cavalry troops here before going into the bloody fray against the Kings men. Master Cromwell was a saintly man who lived his life by his unwavering code of ethics, and sense of what was right, as dictated by the Bible, The two travelling companions shared much with Master Cromwell.

Sir Thomas Fairfax had been appointed with the task of commanding and organising the New Model Army and Oliver Cromwell was now Lt. Gen of the cavalry within that Army. His cavalry troopers were often referred to by the Royalists as Ironsides. Fairfax and Cromwell had certainly changed the course of the war, their innovative tactics and disciplined men spelling disaster for the King's forces.

John had told Matthew that he had heard in Ipswich how Cromwell's troopers were called "Lobsters." When Matthew had asked why they had such a strange name, John laughed as he told him it was on account of the helmets they wore. They had reticulated guards running down the back to protect their necks from the swords of the Cavaliers. These helmets resembled the shell of a lobster! Mathew smiled at John, knowing what he said was not quite right. It was Sir Arthur Haselrig of Leicestershire who had named his troopers Lobsters and not Master Cromwell, but Matthew felt it would be rude and imprudent to correct John. Sometimes John just needed to say or do what he felt was right or what he thought was right or more fundamentally, what he was told was right, this was the state of affairs which best suited Matthew. He knew how to both guide and control his travelling companion.

As they rode in silence Matthew remembered his father James, telling him of the time when this whole exposed area was constantly prone to flooding and how difficult travel had been throughout Norfolk and the surrounding counties. This had changed since the King had granted permission to the Earl of Bedford to try his revolutionary drainage ideas, which had worked better than anyone could have hoped. Now the whole area was miraculously transformed. At least the King had got something right, which proved even misguided men could make some right decisions! John had told him it was all the work of a Dutchman called Sir Cornelius Vermuyden. Matthew already knew this and mused silently on how Vermuyden's son Bartholomew was a Colonel of Horse and served in the New Model Army as part of the Eastern Association alongside Oliver Cromwell. Sometimes, Matthew thought to himself, it was a burden to be constantly alongside people who knew less than he did. After due consideration, he concluded that it was not a belief he held out of arrogance but was just, well, a God given fact.

It was such an unfortunate shame Oliver Cromwell had ordered the re-flooding of whole areas of Fenland to hinder the progress of the Kings men during this period of Civil War. Now it was swiftly returning the area to a bleak landscape of salt marshes, shifting sandbanks and tidal eddies and flows. When the conflict was finally settled, surely the area would once again return to its former state. As his horse plodded ever onwards, stoically negotiating the ruts and muddied puddles in the road, Matthew felt this state of affairs to be a very personal inconvenience, as it impeded him. He allowed his mind to wander but it kept coming back to one thing. Was it too much to ask for? After all he only wanted to be in a warm, dry bed in the port of Kings Lynn before nightfall. This damned war may be fatal to some but it was a damned huge disgraceful inconvenience to him.

This part of the country had been remote and cut off from the rest of England since anyone could remember. You did not travel through the eastern counties to go anywhere else in the land. The exception to this of course was the city of Norwich which was one of the largest cities in England and was very prosperous. Even so, no one just passed through the counties. The result of this lack of outside influence meant the people living here were a very close knit, self-reliant, confidant and private community. This insularity and isolation also created an opportunity for sly, wicked and bad things to incubate, grow and fester unchecked and sometimes undetected.

MATTHEW AND THE KILDERKIN

The evening was drawing in and despite it being summer, the two travellers were already feeling the bite of the cold evening air launching itself towards them on the northern wind as it swept and swirled its way across the waters of the Great Ouse which in turn emptied itself into the Wash. The two men pulled their hats down a little more securely on their heads, bowed forward against the unforgiving offensive of the cooling wind. This weather was not natural for August. Matthew could not shake the subconscious feeling he was travelling towards a diseased place. Securing their cloaks a little tighter, they faced the remaining miles on their weary horses, trudging unremittingly through the inhospitable terrain towards their goal. The summons for them to come to Kings Lynn had arrived in the middle of May. It came from the Mayor, Edward Robinson and was in the form of a letter sent to Matthew by Captain Revett, an alderman at Lynn. The most important thing in the letter as far as Matthew was concerned, was the bold statement, "all charges and recompense would be borne by the Town." This was sweet music to his ears as it meant his fee would be guaranteed and there would be none of that tedious, unseemly and tiresome haggling about his expenses and remuneration once both men had completed their tasks. With the will of God, he might be able to stretch his fee to as much as ten pounds. After all, Matthew and John were the experts; the best there ever had been at their chosen profession. They deserved a payment commensurate to their status.

Matthew and John had been hard at work in St Neots in Cambridgeshire when the summons had arrived. Although the arrival of the letter was welcomed, both men had unfinished business there, which had taken a little while to resolve. But as soon as it had been completed they sent word of their imminent departure from the town and started out on the journey to Lynn.

It was now August and Matthew secretly hoped he could have this whole new episode dealt with inside a few weeks to a month. He had many other places which also required and sought his services. Unknown to Matthew, there was much excited anticipation of the arrival of the two men in the town. As they arrived in the gathering evening gloom they were surprised to find two of Captain Revett's men at the gates to welcome them. There was a trooper on horseback to act as an escort and a drummer on foot, who was enthusiastically beating out to announce the arrival of Matthew and John into Kings Lynn. It became obvious to Matthew, as he revelled in the attention they were receiving upon their entrance into the town, that there might possibly be even more than ten pounds at stake if he provided a satisfactory service. Now their arrival had been well and truly announced, Matthew knew he would have to start his task first thing in the morning. He smiled to himself as soon as he had the thought, performing the Lord's work was never viewed as a task but a necessity. Oh well, no rest for the wicked he mused to himself.

The escort guided them through the chilly evening, giving the men their first glimpse of Lynn. They passed in silence amongst the curious onlookers who were gathering on the streets to see what all the noise and commotion was about. There was still an uneasy peace in the town, which had declared for the Royalist around the outbreak of hostilities in 1643, causing Lynn to be besieged by the Earl of Manchester who stormed the town and restored it to the Parliament. Most townsfolk seeing the group of men ride through their streets knew exactly who their guests were and why they had been summoned to the town. Both Matthew and John had seen the look on these people's faces many times before. The almost reverential glances they received were a mixture of awe and wonderment, augmented of course by looks of dread fear. As the drummer beat their tired passage through the streets, no one seemed to want to look either man directly in the eye or hold their gaze. Faces peeked out of doors held slightly ajar; glances were hurriedly stolen through windows. Hands were held to mouths as whispered conversations took place, fingers were subtly pointed in their direction as they were paraded through the streets behind their escort. Children were taken by the hand and led quickly away by their mothers. There was no cheering, just the watching. Those ever present eyes, both observing and examining the riders as the processed slowly along the gloomy town roads. Those who did look and inadvertently catch the gaze of the riders, deferentially nodded their heads or touched their hats with a respectful forefinger as they passed by the crowds, Matthew and John were high up and felt oddly aloof on their horses plodding ever forward in the descending darkness, now punctuated by lamps in widows, spilling out onto the street. It was not just the weather which brought involuntary shivers to the bodies of some of the on lookers. The two black clad figures of Matthew and John were still swathed in their cloaks against the cold. Their wide brimmed hats covering their heads as they stared stoically to the fore, looking for the world like two dark avenging angels or as some thought, two demons from the pits of hell. Some thought they were as welcome as the plague had been in 1636, though dared not say such a thing publicly.

The small escort eventually arrived with their charges at the welcoming lights of the Inn which would be their home for their stay in the town. Both men dismounted stiffly and wearily, collected their belongings and entered their latest temporary new home. The atmosphere seemed warm and pleasant and they were immediately assured by the landlord, who had magically appeared in front of them, their rooms were the finest in Lynn and their beds were free of fleas. They were told the ale was superb, the food fresh, hot, wholesome and plentiful. He also told the men that he would look after the stabling of their mounts and then they went to the table indicated by their host. The warmth emanating from the fire across the other side of the room was strengthening their host's warm and friendly greeting. The landlord had never really had famous people staying under his roof before, well unless you include those army types like Essex and Cromwell, but as famous as they might be, they just took from the community, they plundered our food, our money, our ale and our men. Usually they returned none of these to their rightful owners. Not the sort of visitors to the town he would like to encourage. These two men were different; they were here to aid the town, its people and the surrounding villages. They were here to give help, not just to take. In these troubled times, this was indeed an unusual occurrence, one which he and many others greatly appreciated. They were very welcome beneath his roof. The two men smiled at each other and after taking food and a little ale, agreed with the landlord's appraisal of his establishment and retired to their rooms.

John Stearne and Matthew Hopkins both settled down for a peaceful night's sleep. The two witchfinders had a long day behind them and an even longer one ahead.

Chapter Two

John and Matthew rose early as was their custom and met for a light breakfast of meats, bread, and small ale. The two men ate contentedly and amid mouthfuls of food they discussed the day ahead. The humour and enthusiasm for life exhibited by the landlord as he had bustled around had been a cheerful start to their day. While bringing them their food he also handed them a note which he had been sent that morning inviting his two guests to the Trinity Guildhall.

They walked the few hundred yards through the busy town and soon came across the magnificent Trinity Guildhall, a black and white chequered building resplendent in the early sunshine. It was certainly a building of some note, nestled within the shadow of St Margaret's church. They were greeted with warmth and affection by the Mayor, Edward Robinson. There were a handful of the town's great, good and Godlie in attendance and formal introductions were quickly dispensed with. Matthew and John had attended many such civic receptions, ostensibly held in their honour. The reality seemed to be it was just an excuse for local people to see their two infamous guests close up. Neither Matthew nor John objected to these occasions, on the contrary in fact they both quite liked the attention their notoriety afforded them. After the formalities had been honoured, Edward Robinson explained to Matthew how there had been little activity of a dark nature in the town or area for the last sixty years. At that time, he recalled, Mother Gabley had caused a ship to sink losing fourteen hands. She did this through the chanting of incantations and the boiling of eggs in a pale full of cold water. The last serious case was almost thirty years ago when Mary Smith stole a hen from Elizabeth Hancocke, who then later fell ill and died after being cursed by her accuser, Henry Smith, a glover. Henry, in jest had apparently accused Elizabeth of stealing his wife Mary's hen. Mary, who was a cheesemonger, repeated the accusation and wished that the bones would stick in Elizabeth's throat if she ate the bird. Afterwards Mary chided Elizabeth, who seems to have fallen ill very soon after. Thankfully Elizabeth did not die and eventually recovered. Mary though had often been involved in disputes with other individuals. Eventually she was hanged for being a witch after she openly admitted she had forsaken God for the Devil. She also confessed to her accusers the Devil had come to her in the shape of a black man and he had also helped her to gain advantage over rivals to her business.

"But now Master Hopkins, we need your help in discovering the witches who are here, right in our midst. We need to stop this latest outbreak of the Devil's work stone dead in its tracks before he gets a hold of other poor souls in our community and rips us asunder."

"What is your evidence for these new occurrences Edward?" inquired Matthew, "and who is involved?"

Edward's face looked both serious and concerned as he continued sombrely, "Matthew, we are on the verge of a plague of

MATTHEW AND THE KILDERKIN

witchery here in the town. Beneath your very feet in the vaults we have eight women and one man who are all accused of witchcraft."

"That is quite a lot of people for one small town," mused John Stearne, "Have they admitted anything of their guilt up to now?" he asked.

"No they have not!" spat Edward Robinson with abrupt indignation, "but be assured gentlemen, we have every confidence your skills will prevail and help us gather the evidence of their guilt."

"Certainly Edward, we are the very people who can do this service for you, if indeed they are guilty of the charges brought before them. With the guiding hand of God, we will discover the truth for you and for the people of Lynn. Before we proceed I must make it clear to you we never accuse anyone of any crime. It is for you as Mayor to decide whether or not allegations brought to your attention by someone within your district should be further investigated. The Devil can be very cunning and witches can be very clever in hiding the truth of their actions, but the truth will always out," said Matthew as he dramatically raised his head and eyes to the heavens, a small silent prayer passed his lips.

Edward went over to the door and opened it, asking Miles Corbett, the Recorder to join them. As Master Corbett entered, Matthew moved forward to greet him asking if he was the same Miles Corbett who did such sterling work in convicting witches in Yarmouth the previous year.

"Indeed it is I Master Hopkins," smiled Corbett, gratified that one as great as Matthew Hopkins had heard of his own modest reputation in helping with the Lord's work. Corbett was obviously a Puritan as was exemplified by his plain unadorned dress of Black shoes, black breeches, white shirt, black doublet and black hat. It was only his hose and shirt which gave slight relief to the dour sobriety of his appearance.

"Please, call me Matthew," smiled Hopkins warmly, taking the man's hand and shaking it vigorously. Half turning he motioned towards John Stearne, "and this is John Stearne, my colleague. John I'd like you to meet Miles Corbett who has the title Inquisitor General," he said as he introduced the two men.

"My pleasure Sir," said Stearne holding forth his outstretched hand and moving towards Corbett. "Please call me John," he said, shaking the proffered hand. "Now pray tell us gentlemen, what awaits us here beneath our feet?" asked John looking back towards the Mayor.

"Sir, we have five widows, Grace Wright, Katherine Banks, Emma Godfrey, Cecily Taylor and Lydia Browne. There are three other women Dorothy Griffin, Thomasine Parker and Dorothy Lee," said Corbett looking down at his papers to refresh his memory. "We also have a male called Thomas Dempster."

"And how are they charged?" asked Matthew looking directly into the eyes of Miles Corbett, who momentarily felt discomfort, unease and was a little in awe of the reputation of Matthew Hopkins.

Miles Corbett lowered his head once more to his sheaf of papers and read, "Sir, they are charged with felonious witchcraft and feloniously consulting and covenanting with an evil spirit."

"And how did they plead?" Matthew questioned, raising an inquisitive eyebrow.

This time the Recorder had no need to look down at his papers. "All nine entered a not guilty plea Matthew and consequently threw themselves on the country," said a solemn Miles Corbett.

"Then we must undertake further investigations into this grave matter," said a thoughtful Hopkins.

Matthew made inquiries as to whether the watchers and searchers assigned to the prisoners had found, seen or heard anything of note while they had been detained whilst awaiting the arrival of the two witchfinders. He was told nothing out of the ordinary had been noticed.

"Then let us descend to your vaults and begin our task," said Matthew leading the way from the room, picking up a lit lantern from a small side table. Matthew was expecting a long descent into vaults which housed gloomy cells, but it seemed there were only a comparatively few short steps leading down into the cellars. These were adjacent to the main door and after what seemed like a brief moment they arrived in a long stone and brick passage way which had doors leading off from it. Both Matthew and John were a little surprised at the conditions here in the vaults. In fact Matthew even remarked to Edward how the atmosphere felt dry. He had been expecting a very dank, fusty and cheerless place.

The prisoners had been separated into three cells, the eight women in two of them, four in each and Thomas Dempster in the third. Rush lights spluttered in their holders on the walls, emitting a weak eerie flickering of shadows. Dark places where the frightened could imagine demons dwelt. It appeared the rush lights had only been lit just before his arrival judging by the rising blue smoke and the pungent smell from the animal fat which they generated as they burned. The smell took Matthew back to his childhood when he was charged with the onerous duty of making them for his own household. Tedious, smelly and boring he remembered. The hours he had spent peeling the rushes so the exposed central pith clung to a solitary strip of rush seemed like such a waste now and then the endless pulling them slowly through the remains of the fat collected from their meals, mutton grease tended to work the best but his favourite time was when he used bacon fat. Matthew loved bacon as a child, the smell was exquisite. Then when they had been drawn several times through the rendered fat he would lay them out to dry and tie them into neat bundles for his mother to use around the house. His mother frequently gave him a small amount of beeswax to add to his mixture as this improved the quality of the light and elongated the life of the rush lamp. Each rush candle was about a foot long and generally lasted about 15 minutes. The children in the household used to take it in turns changing them in the corridors and rooms of the house where they were burned. Everyone hated this job. Often to gain a little more light they would burn the candle at both ends.

Matthew awoke from his reminiscence and took a cursory glance through the small barred window in each wooden door as he slowly passed them. There were two other free rooms in the vaults and Hopkins asked for a table and chairs to be placed in them so he and John Stearne could speak to the suspects in privacy. He also asked for more light to be made available in them. While this was being arranged he was introduced to the three goodwives who had been acting as the watchers and searchers over the last few months. They seemed like three Godlie and conscientious women and Matthew knew their testimony would be invaluable at the forthcoming trial. He had sent his own watcher, Mary Phillips ahead of John and himself to train the other women and gaolers as to signs they should be looking out for. He was acutely aware that as Godlie as they might appear, they had not had any previous experience dealing with the demons and Devils which may be

MATTHEW AND THE KILDERKIN 19

lurking within the prisoners. It was the responsibility of the goodwives to observe, eavesdrop and make notes of what they saw and heard. The three ladies took equal shifts under the tutelage of Mary Phillips. They were tasked with sitting on a chair placed for their comfort in the passageway adjacent to the cell doors, waiting, watching and listening. Matthew had seen the Devil in all his guises and was very well aware how he could conceal and hide himself. What the women might now witness would see them in good stead for the future. Matthew always felt it was good for more people within a community to be able spot the signs of the Devil and know where to look and more importantly to be able to interpret what they saw.

"John, you take the women in that cell and I'll take the women in that one," indicated Hopkins with a nod of his head. "While you make a start, I'll go and make the acquaintance of Master Dempster." Miles Corbett and one of the goodwives followed Matthew to the door at the end of the corridor. Here Corbett proceeded to act as turnkey and when the door was unlocked he politely stood aside and held it open for Matthew to enter. The Witchfinder lowered his head as he moved through the low door holding his lantern at arm's length before him as he entered the cell. The cell was quite clean and pleasant, not at all what Matthew was expecting, evidently the town of Lynn treated their prisoners with an uncommon courtesy. The smell was even tolerable. There was no natural light and the ubiquitous rush light stuttered and guttered in a holder on the wall. By contrast the brighter candle light radiating from his own lantern was more than enough for Matthew to witness a very weary, yet wary looking Thomas Dempster who was sat on the floor. Matthew immediately saw the fear in the man's eyes behind the bravado he would surely attempt to portray. Corbett had previously told Matthew how Dempster had been subjected to running by his watchers. The running up and down his cell and the passageway beyond its door had kept him from his sleep for several nights in a row. He had been forced to run backwards and forwards until Dempster was out of breath. After a brief rest, the male watchers from the town guard would run him again. This was repeated for several days and nights until he was weary of his life and he hardly knew what he said or did, or even cared. He had just wanted it to stop. Running was one of Matthew's most frequently used methods to gain a confession. It had not worked in this case.

"Stand up Dempster!" snapped Corbett, moving across the room and roughly kicking Thomas in the thigh. With a sharp intake of breath Thomas took the blow and stood up while rubbing his leg to ease the sudden pain of the kick. Matthew also noticed how behind the eyes there flared a brief spark of defiance. I'll have to be careful with this one thought Matthew as he slowly walked around the figure standing before him. Although he had been kept for months in this darkened place and had not enjoyed the healthiest of diets, Matthew could see Dempster was a fit man who was still powerful. This obviously explained the reason why he was chained securely to the wall by his ankle.

"Do you know who this is?" shouted Corbett. Not waiting for a reply, he immediately continued, "This is the man who will watch you hang. Yes, hang Dempster, you will hang while we all watch you turn blue and see your tongue loll out of the corner of your mouth while everyone will laugh at your jerking thrashing body on the end of the rope. We will watch as you piss and shit your pants." Corbett was obviously enjoying this form of bullying. "This gentleman before you is the enemy of Satan, furthermore this is the man who will reveal the very Devil in you," snarled Corbett, now totally enthused by his theme. "This is the Witchfinder; Matthew Hopkins, and he has travelled far to come here today to release you from the grip of the Devil. This he will do by God's divine will."

By the time Corbett had finished his tirade; Matthew had slowly circled Dempster and returned to stand in front of him. He noticed the prisoner had paled considerably during Corbett's speech and had bowed his head. "Yes Dempster, as you jerk on the end of the rope and the shit runs down your legs you will be an ugly thing which only the Devil would want to care for." To Corbett it felt naturally good to not only intimidate and frighten the wretched man he had before him but to also impress his guest with his vim and vigour as he pressed the case. "As you draw your last gasp of God's good clean air, even he will forsake you, leaving you and your soul to Old Nick to torment at his leisure, a torment which will last for all eternity." Corbett emphasized the point by cruelly stamping on Dumpster's right toes making the prisoner yell with pain and hop about trying to get some relief from the searing pain he had just experienced. "See how that makes you dance and leap about Thomas; trust me, it is nothing compared to what you will experience whilst dangling in the air at the end of a coarse and rude length of hemp. When you have breathed your last, your evil pact with the Devil will become complete. It will only be at that point your soul will begin to experience all the pains and trials of hell and your personal ordeal with Satan will really begin." Corbett waited a minute or so in silence to let his words sink in. No one moved or made a sound in the cell; the only noise was the quickened breath of the prisoner. "Do you know what will happen then Dempster, do you have any idea?" Corbett paused, waiting for a reply, which did not come. Matthew looked at the ashen faced prisoner and Corbett answered his own question which had been left hanging in the air. "No? Then I will tell you. We will all go to the Inn and have beer and a hearty breakfast. We will be alive and you will be dead and beginning your perpetual torment in the depths of hell."

Silence reigned, not a word was uttered by anyone. Thomas looked up into the eyes of both men, now plainly terrified with his tears freely flowing from his eyes and making tracks down across his un-washed cheeks. In that one instant Matthew could tell the man was clearly repentant and genuinely scared.

"Thank you for so vividly painting Master Dempster's future. Would you leave us alone now please Master Corbett?" said Matthew nodding Miles towards the door.

Corbett took the hint and left the room. "I will prepare your room for you sir." He said as he left and turned along the corridor. Matthew watched as Miles Corbett left the room and then turned and looked Dempster directly in the eyes, "It does not have to be like this Thomas," said Matthew gently. "All I need from you is your testimony of guilt and your repentance."

Matthew stood silently before Thomas waiting for him to speak. "I am innocent Sir, I have done nothing wrong," pleaded Thomas, the tracks of his tears reflecting in the lamplight.

"Then why are you here? How have you found yourself in this awful place facing such a fate? Tell me Thomas, have you ever attended the execution of a convicted witch?" asked Matthew.

"No sir, I have not," replied Thomas through still watering eyes and wiping his running nose on his sleeve. Matthew could see the spark of defiance had receded and had become once again buried, overshadowed by fear. Although he did not approve of Master Corbett's methods he found himself grateful to him because he had now given Matthew the opportunity to make Thomas feel he had befriended him. Matthew was happy to use any recourse which ended with the truth being uncovered through the line of least resistance.

"Well Thomas, as I'm sure you will understand I have attended many. For some people they are joyous occasions, for others they are very sad, for others nothing more than a way of making money. Did you know Thomas, rooms around the execution area are rented out for people to watch the spectacle, and carpenters, along with other enterprising people, build platforms rising above the heads of others so they can have an unimpeded view of the proceedings. I am sickened when I see people selling shoddy trinkets of the occasion, dolls with pins in them or small ropes and nooses or even little wooden gallows for the children play with. You can usually buy kerchiefs dipped in the sweat of the victim or sometimes small squares of the witches clothing. This time it will be your sweat and your clothing Thomas. How do you think that will make your family and friends feel?"

The Witchfinder continued with his diatribe, "Thomas what do you think the last thing you will hear might be? Will it be a sharp intake of breath from the crowd as you begin your drop to hell, will it be the last words of the priest, or maybe even the cry of a loved one rising above the hushed silence of the onlookers or even the crack of the breaking bones in your neck. Let me enlighten you Thomas." Here Matthew took a dramatic pause.

"None of these sounds will be the last thing you will hear." Silence reigned as these words were left hanging in the air of the room.

"It will be the overwhelming sounds of disinterest. It will be the sounds of the bawdy drunks in the taverns who are laughing along with their friends. Most people will have travelled into the town from the surrounding villages, not to see a witch die but because there will be a gathering of their friends in the ale houses and fine pies and victuals will be on sale and they will want to join in the atmosphere of a fayre. They will have come to Lynn with the full intention of witnessing your execution and those of the women, but somehow or other they will get waylaid by long lost friends or food and ale and they will usually forget to walk the last few paces to the execution site because they might lose their places in the food queues or their seats in the taverns and ale houses. People will be queuing to buy souvenirs of the occasion, instead of watching the actual event. Yes Thomas, mark my words, the last thing you will hear will be disinterest and total indifference. You may recognise a bawdy song or a new ballad being sung through an open window, your death will be meaningless to everyone. There will be no sounds of wailing or sobbing at your death, no one will be there shouting for your release or protesting your innocence, no one. Your family and friends will not be present as they will be ashamed of you or may not wish to be seen to be associated with a convicted and proven witch, who is about to begin a sentence of eternal writhing in the fires of hell".

"The only people who will care about you and your mortal soul will be you, God and Matthew Hopkins."

Matthew watched Thomas's shoulders droop and the tears start once again as he imagined the picture Matthew painted. He felt utterly alone, miserable and rejected. "I am the only person who can help you Thomas and I can only do this thing if you help me, and of course if God in his infinite wisdom, shows me the way. Who will be there to watch you die Thomas, who will be there to weep? Do you have any family or loved ones?"

MATTHEW AND THE KILDERKIN 25

Thomas felt devastated by these words and he realised Matthew was indeed his only hope of escaping the gallows and for his everlasting salvation. "I have no family Master Hopkins and I have only ever loved two women, both widows and they have both loved me, the trouble is they are sharing a cell next door, Grace Wright and Emma Godfey."

Matthew turned away from Thomas and involuntarily raised his eyebrow, so this man has communed with two other witches was his first and immediate thought. By his own mouth he will convict them if he is indeed guilty or they him, if they are guilty.

"So you have two women who care for you and have both loved you. They are also unfortunate enough to find themselves here in this awful place," said Hopkins to a quiet, compliant and defeated Dempster.

"Yes sir, I used to lie with Grace some ten years hence and then I met Emma and stopped seeing Grace. I care for them both and they are both as innocent as I Sir"

"Or as guilty!" said Matthew raising his voice and looking Thomas straight into the eyes with his cold unfeeling, grim stare. "We shall see Master Dempster, we shall see. Either I or John Stearne will tease out all your secrets one way or another. Or maybe I should pass you into the hands of Master Corbett, I think he might like to try to find the truth which is hidden deep inside your soul Thomas, after all he proved very able and accomplished at doing that job whilst in Yarmouth. "What do you think Thomas?"

Thomas knew very well about Miles Corbett's reputation, he understood if you came before him then your days were pretty well numbered, unless you had power, influence or money. Thomas was in short supply of any of those commodities. All he had were his wits and his muscles. He had always managed to earn his own living, have fun and be beholden to no living soul. Miles Corbett was a man to be truly feared, some say more so than Matthew Hopkins. He was a zealot and loved his work finding witches, some say he loved it far too much and behaved more like the hangman than the hangman himself. "Bloody puritans," he thought to himself. If you came before Corbett in his capacity as Recorder, the least you would probably get away with was a good whipping, innocent or not and for a more serious offence, if you had no goods or chattels, you would almost certainly hang. It was said the worst murderer in the land could buy his way from the gallows if Corbett was sitting in judgement. Thomas realised his position was precarious and he had nothing with which to strike a bargain with Miles Corbett. Things were now even worse and more hopeless, if indeed such a thing were possible as Matthew Hopkins was now in charge. He also realised, as did Matthew, how one utterance of a wrong word from either Grace or Emma and the fate of all three would sealed.

Then an idea came to him.

Chapter Three

Their morning's work had been fruitful and confessions had been readily forthcoming to John Stearne from both Dorothy Lee and Grace Wright. John, like Matthew was constantly surprised at how easily some people would let others see the demons lurking within them and confess their sins. Lydia Browne he was unsure of. Stearne thought Matthew had better speak to her and give his opinion. The Devil's marks had been found on Dorothy Griffin by one of the goodwife searchers, Mary Phillips, along with a mark which needed further interpretation which was discovered on the upper thigh of Emma Godfrey. It also seemed the other women who Matthew and John had interviewed were weakening in their stories. It only needed one of them to confess and the truth about all the others would come tumbling out. Their stories would collapse like a house of cards. John and Matthew felt pleased with their mornings work as they sat in the Inn ruminating and discussing the interviews they had already conducted. Cross referencing and comparing all the details they had been told as they ate. There were many apparent discrepancies and flaws in the stories and as Matthew knew only too well, you only needed to find one loose end of a story and start picking and before very long, the whole sorry tale would unravel.

They had adjourned to the Inn where they were enjoying cold roast beef, bread, cheeses and foaming tankards of ale. As they ate and drank they both agreed, just as the landlord had boasted, the victuals were of the highest quality. The few other people enjoying their food at the Inn kept a respectful distance from the two notorious witchfinders but their eyes were constantly flicking over towards the two men.

It was resolved that for their afternoons work, John would inspect the marks found on Emma Godfrey and Dorothy Griffin by the searcher and confirm their presence and Matthew would talk to Dorothy Lee and Lydia Brown, to confirm the confession of Mistress Lee and make an opinion about Mistress Brown. He would then have another talk with Master Dempster.

When Matthew and John returned to the cells in the vaults beneath the Trinity Guildhall they separated, going into their own rooms. Matthew left Stearne preparing the equipment for his invasive inspections of the two women he was to question.

Matthew entered the room and stood still, an involuntary grin sweeping across his face. It became apparent now as to what Miles Corbett had meant when he told him earlier he would prepare the room for his esteemed guest. There on the table, sat five huge beeswax candles, causing the room to seem ablaze with light. Presumably he had requested them to be sent over from St Margaret's church opposite the Guildhall. He also noticed there was a small barred window in the room, high up but no light seemed to penetrate through it. Matthew guessed it was purely there for ventilation. The table was towards the rear wall of the cell, for that is what Matthew judged the room to be used as under normal circumstances and the candles were clumped together in the centre of the table. Their combined melted wax had made a stable base for them in which to reside. There were three chairs, one on his side of the small plain wooden table and one facing towards him allowing him to look into the faces of the accused as he interviewed them. Behind that again was a third chair against the wall where the goodwife would sit. The stone and brick room was completed by a noose which had been attached to a spike hammered into a beam above the seat where the prisoners would sit. Matthew thought this was very childish and theatrical and once again smiled at the daunting sight which would greet his prisoners as they entered the cell. Miles Corbett may well be the MP for Yarmouth but he certainly knew how to aid the extraction of a confession. Matthew was half tempted to stand on the chair and remove it. He was not keen on cheap theatrics but then decided to leave it be, after all it was not him who had put it there and therefore could not be held responsible for the added intimidation. Matthew went to the door and looked down the corridor to where the gaoler and a couple of other people stood quietly chatting and called for Dorothy Lee to be brought to him.

When she arrived, she was being supported by both the gaoler and a goodwife, Mary Phillips, the searcher he often employed. Mary was a widow and also lived in Manningtree. Matthew had often employed her to go before him to conduct searches on his behalf. Mary was good at her job and Matthew appreciated having at least one searcher he could rely upon to find the things and ask the questions which searchers with little or no experience from the local community did not ask. He motioned for them to place her in the chair. He could see the months spent in the prison and the poor diet, had taken their toll. He silently hoped the trial would be set soon, lest she should die beforehand. The gaoler left and closed the door and the goodwife, Phillips sat a few feet behind Dorothy.

Dorothy sat still with her head hanging lifelessly over her chest. Matthew could see her erratic breaths making her chest rise and fall. This was a woman at the end of her tether.

"Dorothy, can you hear me?" asked Matthew. "Dorothy can you hear me?" he repeated, this time a little louder and more insistent. The goodwife got up from her chair behind her charge and yanked Dorothy's head roughly backwards by the hair and spat venomously into her ear, "Master 'opkins is a talking to you witch, you'd better chat to 'un an double quick about it."

With her hair pulling her head back, Matthew could see how she had dried patches of blood beneath her nose and an eye which was darkening. Although her eyes were closed and puffy through many hours of crying, he noticed them begin to focus as they alighted on the noose above her head. She saw it but did not seem to recognise its significance. He could see at one time in the past Dorothy had been of a fair countenance. Matthew observed the tell-tale blood reddened pock marks around her shoulders, running down her chest under her bodice showing where John had pricked her earlier in the day. Of course if during the pricking of a Devils mark, no pain or bleeding occurred, this was not enough evidence on its own to convict but added weight to subsequent further evidence which may be gathered. The marks were usually where the Devil had either scraped his claw over a part of the body or had licked it with his tongue. Matthew knew the Devil to be crafty fiend and he usually tried to hide his mark, sometimes it might take the guise of a scar or a birth mark or sometimes an extra nipple or even a mole. Sometimes he would hide them deep inside a woman's most private parts. Oh, yes, he was crafty alright. All had to be inspected and pricked with equal vigour. Those which yielded no blood nor made the suspect cry out in pain were noted.

Stearne and the goodwife had found such a mark on Dorothy's hip. Matthew had heard tales of some witchfinders using witch prickers, instruments of inspection where the spike could be retracted up inside the handle at the pressing of a secret button, thus of course causing no pain at all to the prisoner. These helped the witchfinder gain a conviction. Matthew and John were disgusted at such tales and would never resort to such underhanded, illegal and dishonest methods, there was no need to. They were both very proficient at their task.

Dorothy Lee slowly opened her empty eyes and looked vacantly in Matthew's direction. "Tell me Dorothy have you communed with the Devil?" asked the Witchfinder. There was no reply. Matthew took another tack, stood up and walked around the room before continuing, "I hear you have a cat called Boy, is that correct Dorothy?" Dorothy appeared to recognise the name and said quietly, as if to her-self, "Boy."

"Is it true he sleeps in your bed Dorothy?" asked Matthew, "I have been told you have been seen flying through the night sky with Boy, is that right Dorothy?"

"Boy is my friend, my companion," whispered Dorothy in a broken voice, quietly sobbing. "He travels everywhere with me, he is my very best friend, he is always at my side, I love him."

"There!" exclaimed the goodwife, rising in her seat and pointing animatedly at the prisoner sitting in front of her. "From 'er own lips Master 'opkins, you 'eard her, you ast 'er if she could fly and 'er said wherever she goes 'ee goes. Ast er if Boy can fly, if 'ee cant then she must be able to take 'un. From 'er own lips Master 'opkins I eard 'er, 'ee be 'er familiar, an' she even takes 'im to 'er bed!" The goodwife, Mary Phillips was beside her-self with rage.

Returning his attention to Dorothy Lee after the unexpected outburst he continued in a calmer tone, "Dorothy, I have been told you placed a curse on Mrs Watkins, would you tell me why you did such a thing?" Dorothy opened her eyes wide and looked at Matthew and simply said in a firm and determined voice "She deserved it, I saw her kick Boy, she made the Devil rise in me when I saw her do it and so I cursed her."

"Do you know what you are saying Dorothy?" asked Matthew.

"Yes she does sir," said the goodwife, "I 'eard 'er say the Devil rose up in her and she cursed Mrs Watkins, why it made the poor wummans cow give sour milk and then Mr Watkins chopped off two fingers when 'ee were cutting firewood, 'ee said the axe just seemed to take on a life of its own and landed across 'is 'and Sir! I know 'e'll swear to that Sir. I just 'eard 'er say all those words Sir, I'll testify for you against 'er and be jolly pleased to be doin' my part"

Matthew was about to continue when a weak voice said, "Yes I hate her. I wish her ill, she hurt poor Boy and he had done nothing to her at all, nothing." Dorothy wept, her shoulders rising and falling as she did so, her eyes closed tightly and the tears escaped and seeped down onto her cheeks.

The goodwife violently thrust Dorothy's head forward back down on to her chest as she let go of Dorothy's hair. "Guilty as sin Sir, I knew she were a bad 'un when I first clapped eyes on 'er. I were told by some of the folks here that even when she were younger she were trouble, but nobody never dreamt she were in league with Satan Master Hopkins. Well now we know all about you Dorothy Lee!" she spat the words contemptuously, eyeing the sobbing woman with no sign of compassion.

"I fear so," said Hopkins as he crossed himself. He had heard enough for himself and in the presence of a witness and with the evidence supplemented by the testimony to be submitted by Stearne, she would surely hang. "Tell me Widow Phillips, how did she get the swollen eye and the blood under her nose?" asked Hopkins turning his attention from Dorothy to the goodwife.

"She become a bit agitated Sir and the gaoler and me decided her 'ad to be settled down before I took 'er to see Master Stearne this mornin'. She didn't want to go and kicked up a fuss, so I 'ad to 'elp 'er along a bit, if you knows what I mean, you know, calm 'er down a bit. It worked, Master 'opkins, she went quiet as a lamb in the end."

Matthew glowered at the goodwife and lowered his voice into the most menacing she had ever heard and whispered, "If you ever treat one of my prisoners like that again, you will find yourself swapping places with her, do you understand goodwife?" Hopkins did not give her the chance to reply before bellowing, "Do you understand!" Both Dorothy and the goodwife jumped. "Now take her away and bring me Lydia Browne." Hopkins knew confessions extracted through torture were sorely frowned upon in some circles and if this unjustifiable treatment of prisoners continued, he could lose both his fee and his reputation. Widow Phillips should have known better. Secretly, he was also a little pleased the goodwife had meted out some "persuasion" in front of the other prisoners in the cell as it would make them realise it was better to co-operate with Masters Hopkins and Stearne than not. The gaoler was called for and he and the goodwife led Dorothy back to her cell.

Matthew made a few notes of the interview in the bright steady candlelight. After a couple of minutes there was a knock at the door and Lydia Browne was led into the room shackled but walking ably between the gaoler and widow Phillips, who this time took her seat rather sheepishly at the back of the room. As soon as she sat down

Lydia's eyes were all over the room and she looked as excited as a child receiving gifts. Lydia was a thin tall, wiry, straggly looking woman who Matthew judged to be in her late fifties or early sixties. Her eyes looked alert and she had a lively step even though she was shackled. Her long unkempt grey hair made her look every inch the witch she was accused of being.

"That's a nice hat sir," she said quickly, "My goodness you are a handsome gentleman, Master Hopkins, so tall, I like that in a man. I bet you run the girls ragged," she sniggered. "Call me Lydia sir, can I call you Matthew? Why, you have got big hands Matthew, you know what they say about men with big hands don't you," she laughed teasingly. Before Matthew could respond, she quickly carried on, "I hate this place Matthew. Can you get me out? I'll do anything you ask of me." She looked lasciviously at Matthew Hopkins, running her tongue across her lips, "just get this old whore behind me to leave," she flicked her head backwards in the direction of the goodwife, "and you can do whatever you want to me, anything at all. Just let me go. I won't tell nobody neither. You can trust me Matthew, I might be a bit old but I know what to do. I can still bring a smile to a young man's face and I can see you are a real man Matthew, yes a real man of the world," she said as she sat before him. She then opened her thighs as wide as the shackles would allow, "it is yours if you want it Matthew," She turned her head and her eyes then travelled wantonly to the goodwife and after looking her up and down, returned to Hopkins. "She can watch us if you like, would you like her to watch? It doesn't bother me; it might even be nice if she joined in."

Matthew noticed the widow Phillips blush deeply, but after his words to her a few minutes ago, she kept her countenance. He had heard everything in his years of witchfinding and this was nothing new, he smiled inwardly at the haste of her speech, at this rate he would not be able to get a word in edge ways.

"I've got powerful friends you know Matthew, Master Cromwell his self is a friend of mine and I know the Pope, we were special friends if you gets my drift," she said winking at her inquisitor. I also knowed the King of France, a good friend to me he is." Her face spread into a self-satisfied smile, "Matthew, I bet you didn't know I knew all those people when I came into this room did you. Important I am. Rich as well, I could give you all my money if you let me go in peace, worth hundreds I am Matthew, hundreds I tell you. That's right isn't it, go on you can tell him, he is our friend aren't you Matthew," as she was saying this she was turning her head towards the opposite wall of the room and the remark made Matthew jump for a moment, he thought someone had entered and Lydia Browne was addressing them, but Matthew turned his head and looked in the direction and just saw the wall. All he could see were indistinct shadows being cast by the gently flickering light.

"Who are you talking to Lydia?" asked Matthew returning his gaze to the woman before him.

"Why, to him Matthew," she said, nodding her head in the direction of the wall and wide eyed in surprise that Matthew could not see anyone there. "Don't you see him? He's my friend, my very bestest and closest friend. He just told me he would like to watch you have your will with me Matthew. He likes watching me making men happy. Oh, I'm sorry, my manners are slipping," Her voice changed to a more formal one, as if introducing strangers to each other in a church. "Matthew, this is Nick; Nick this is Matthew, my new friend." Her voice returned to normal and she carried on unabated, "Nick was my first husband Matthew, before I met

Charlie Stuart you understand." Her gaze returned once more to the Witchfinder, "Old Nick don't always understand Matthew, but he is my friend and he helps me when I get angry with people, I chats to him and things happen to them. Bad things, but only what they deserve mind! Nick is a very handy friend to have Matthew." She then leaned forward, looked behind herself to make sure the goodwife was still sat down and whispered very quietly, "I have told him to look after you though, I don't want anything to happen to you, after all we did love each other at one time didn't we."

Matthew had seen women like this before; she was totally mad and belonged in Bethlem, down there in Bishopsgate, not inside a prison cell. This would be simple he thought to himself, she would be asked a few simple questions and she would hang herself with the responses. The people of Lynn wanted a witch or two to dangle and after all, it was they and not Matthew who had charged Lydia Browne with witchcraft, and Matthew did, after all, have a job to do. He knew he had to ask her a couple of questions which would ensure the noose would tighten around her neck.

"Lydia, how long have you known Nick?"

""Why bless you Matthew, all my life of course. Old Nick and me have been lovers since I was a child, in fact he was my first," she remembered thoughtfully. "Even before my brother, I was six," she added helpfully.

"Tell me Lydia, does Nick have any other names or friends who he brings to meet you sometimes?" asked Matthew guessing at the response.

"Of course he brings his friends, little imps they are too, always up to no good, hiding under my skirts and being rude with my nether parts. I have to tell you though Matthew, I like that." She winked at him and smiled at the recollection, "but they also help me when I want to put a curse on someone who might have hurt me. Matthew, between you and me, I have to confess they can be a bit bothersome and a real nuisance sometimes, but they are still my friends. Nick has many names, sometimes he makes me call him Master, he likes that, he says it shows I respect him. He sometimes commands me to call him Satan but I think that makes him sound unfriendly, don't you? I prefer it when he tells me to call him Bill, I like the name Bill; all friendly like. It was my uncle's name you know. He was a nice man." Her eyes seemed to glaze over with a dreamy far-away look, "My uncle Bill used to live on the moon with a cow, he could jump up there every night you know, and he was married to my aunty Mary. She was the Queen of Scotland." Lydia seemed to refocus her eyes and continued, "Don't look at me like that, it's true, I'm not lying you know. Royalty is in my family and runs freely in my blood. Did you know that Matthew? You can see it in my face can't you." She majestically and slowly turned her head from left to right, allowing the Witchfinder to inspect her profile. She beamed with pride and said, "There you are, you can see it now can't you Sir!"

"Bill sounds like a nice name Lydia, you prefer that to Old Nick do you?" asked Hopkins quietly.

""Yes I do, it is our little joke, me calling him Bill, he actually tells me to call him Bill Zeebub, but I just call him Bill, don't I Bill?" she smiled affectionately as she looked towards the wall.

Matthew could see the look of horror on the face of the goodwife sat nervously behind Lydia, "Did you hear and understand her answers, goodwife?"

"Yes I did Sir; 'er is in league with the Devil 'imself Sir. I'll testify wot I 'eard in 'ere today." The goodwife looked troubled and then continued confiding, "I'm afeard though Sir. Will he get my soul? Old Nick I mean, what with me 'elping you and all Master 'opkins?" said the goodwife with a look of fear spreading across her face.

Matthew Hopkins smiled at the goodwife's look of foreboding and at the same time felt sympathy for the poor deranged woman who sat babbling before him. "I think you will be fine Mary, we will go to church and pray together later. I think the dark power which Lydia Browne once had has now departed since the Lord has entered her heart and forced her to tell the truth to us today, we are privileged goodwife to witness her confession, words which have flowed freely after having been pried from her heart and lips by the grace of our good Lord."

"The Lord, the good Lord, good Lord, the Lord is my shepherd, I shall not want," Lydia said and then she stopped and thought about the words she had just said and continued, "I don't want anything from him Matthew." Lydia appeared to Matthew to be rambling incoherently, she continued, "Matthew did I tell you that earlier? About the good shepherd I mean?" She had a look of lost bewilderment across her face, and then seemed to collect her thoughts and carried on. "When I was a lost sheep he found me you know, up on the hills, when I was living in a place called Heaven, before I come to Kings Lynn it was, I was just feeding from the sweet, green wet grass and the shepherd found me and told me to join his flock. Of course Bill had other ideas. I did like being a sheep though, the Lord made me feel nice when he was my shepherd, he was the one what lied with me beside the still waters, well, this was before the fisherman gentleman called Peter came along looking for souls. Now, there was another handsome man, he told me he knew Jesus and had a cock that could do something three times before the morning came and he would show it to me, or something like that, I forget now, it was a long time ago, I get a bit confusculated sometimes, but Bill always comes and talks to me and gives me advice. He said he will keep me warm forever when my body dies. I don't like the cold Matthew, so a hot place with Bill sounds glorious and I can be with all my other friends, the imps and demons."

Unable to contain herself any longer Mary Phillips shouted, "She blasphemes!" leaning forward she swiped the woman with a stinging slap around the back of her head.

"No, she is mad," whispered Matthew to himself.

Chapter Four

Matthew pondered as the gaoler and the goodwife walked Lydia Browne back to her cell. He knew she would probably hang, but he also knew she was clearly mad and not possessed by the Devil but then again, what was possession if not a form of deluded madness?

Thomas Dempster was still sat on the floor of his cell when Matthew entered. "Good afternoon Master Hopkins," said Thomas as he got to his feet and bowed his head. The two men were alone in the cell.

"My colleague John Stearne, found what could be the Devils mark on the body of Emma Godfrey earlier today Thomas. You know this may be evidence of her being a witch and by your own admission you have lain with both her and Grace Wright, who is also here charged with the same crime. You are in trouble Thomas. Your guilt is assured," said Matthew in a frighteningly cold, steely, dispassionate, yet even tempered voice.

Matthew then remained silent and stood looking unwaveringly into the eyes of the man before him. He saw the expression on the face of Dempster change from one of deference to one of anxiety and then to the expression of a man who has just seen his future and does not want to acknowledge the inevitable fate which awaits him. Thomas knew in his heart this moment signalled the end for him.

His mind raced, he had formulated a plan to put to Matthew Hopkins. Since their initial meeting this morning he had been studiously working it through but events had moved quicker than he had anticipated and now he suddenly felt frantic and very scared. He concluded his only chance was to try and convince Hopkins of a half told secret he had once heard while sharing the pillow of Grace Wright. He would try anything to save his life. No matter how futile. He did not want to hang in public like a piece of butchers meat and let his body be the subject of other people's cruel jokes and barbed comments.

"Please Master Hopkins, listen to me. I have a story to tell you." Matthew had seen many a prisoner react in this way to try and extricate themselves from their position. Next would be the offer of a bribe, then the threats of retaliation from family or friends then the pleading and tears and finally the acceptance of their inevitable fate. God had made Matthew strong and impervious to these protestations and temptations. These moments were always his personal trials.

"You wish to confess your covenanting with an evil spirit?" asked Matthew.

"No sir, of that I am innocent, but I have a strange tale to relate to you. One which involves a lost wealth, which if recovered, would enable you to do much good for the church and likewise the Commonwealth. It could also enable you to help the people of England during these troubled wars. Should you make this discovery it would make you a man who would be revered, not only for your work in finding witches, but would make you one of England's greatest men. Monies would also be secured for you

MATTHEW AND THE KILDERKIN 43

and *your* future generations which will follow, enabling them to continue to carry out God's work." Thomas spoke in slow measured tones.

This was the gamble of his life. In just a few sentences Thomas had to try and appeal to Hopkins's commitment, standing, fervour, honour, and greed, all in equal measures. Thomas was a simple man and had earned his living by his own hands and honest labour, but he knew of the importance of words and was hoping he had judged not only his words but his reading of Matthew Hopkins. The next few seconds and Matthew's reaction would forever seal his fate.

Matthew had heard this type of thing before, it sounded as pathetic as the rush-light sputtering in its holder, trying desperately to cast sufficient light into the gloom of the cell. It was usually couched in a more direct manner. Statements of this fashion were designed to appeal to his personal greed and usually came attached to a figure, usually a few pounds at most. This sounded different, it was not a direct bribe but was about information and Dempster had pointed out to Matthew the good he could do with a considerable sum of money. He surmised Dempster could not be talking about a few pounds as he had inferred a large enough sum to facilitate influence on both the church and the country.

Matthew could not help but be intrigued. "Continue," he said quietly.

"Sir it is an account of fantastic proportions. Before I start on my tale, I have just one thing only to ask of you."

Hopkins smiled and thought to himself there is always just "one thing" to be asked of him. "Let me guess Thomas, might it be the one thing you request is for me to free you?"

Thomas realised immediately his mistake and how crudely childish the request would appear to a gentleman like Matthew

Hopkins. Surely he would just scoff at his clumsy attempt towards liberty and regard him as yet another in a long line of desperate men and women who will say anything to be free of the hangman's hemp. Thomas knew instantly he would have no other choice but to change his plan and throw himself on the mercy of Hopkins. So he immediately decided to change tack. He hoped his assessment of the Witchfinder's character might prove to be correct.

"Of course I don't wish to die Sir, but before God, I swear to you I am innocent of any charges brought before me. My maker will affirm the purity of my actions on judgement day. I have no wish to go to the scaffold but I know if it is to be the case, my soul will be in God's hands and not those of the Devil. I am innocent Master Hopkins." Thomas delivered these words in a steady and determined voice, brimming with both conviction and sincerity. "No sir, the thing I ask of you is that if these riches and power fall into your hands, you use them wisely and for the good of all people. My wish is you leave a legacy for the others who will follow us. I know Master Hopkins you are a good and righteous man and you can easily see right from wrong. Indeed Sir, the way you have been called to lead your life can only show you to be a true instrument of God, steadfastly doing his labours here on earth. I know if you secure these great riches, your future deeds will be for the good of all. I can think of no one else during these foul and pestilent civil wars that could or would do more. Master Hopkins, if the tale I tell you is proven to be as true and honest as your heart and you find yourself guided by the hand of God I know it will lead you to find Emma Godfrey, Grace Wright and I, Thomas Dempster free and innocent of the malicious slanders and indictments levelled against us. We are all three, innocent as I stand here before you in God's eyes. If it be God's will, then I know we will all be acquitted, if not

MATTHEW AND THE KILDERKIN

then we will surely hang." Thomas stopped speaking and silently prayed his words might be enough to encourage Matthew to listen to more of his tale.

Matthew turned and slowly walked around the prisoner, ruminating on Dempster's impassioned words. Once again, he was intrigued by his plea for Matthew to do good with any money which might fall into his possession. Matthew was also gratified with Dempster's acknowledgement regarding the fate of his two lovers and his own life, being in God's hands and not his own. He surmised Thomas was appealing to his higher morals and vanity, but all that to one side, if there was a small fortune hidden away somewhere, it might be worth discovering. After all, he could do a lot of good with a hundred pounds or so. "Continue," said Matthew as he returned to stand once more before his charge.

"I will start at the beginning sir. I told you I used to walk out with Grace Wright and we were lovers. Marriage was imminent, until I met Emma and then my heart went out to her and I realised what true love was." I loved Grace with all my heart but after I met Emma, my world changed forever.

"Get on with it!" snapped Hopkins, beginning to weary of this yarn already.

"Forgive me sir, well Grace and I spent numerous nights in each other's arms and many of those nights were spent after a visit to the ale house. On one such occasion we were talking in bed and she told me of a family secret, one which she told me she had never uttered before to another soul. The secret had been passed down from her father and his father before him and many times before that. It was a story of a treasure hoard, whispered to be many hundreds of years old. Riches which I was told had been discovered by a long dead ancestor. Well Master Hopkins although Grace was in her cups and rambled a bit I knew I had to be careful, I needed to be very delicate in guiding the direction of the conversation with her," said Thomas. All the while Thomas Dempster was looking into Matthews face, trying to gauge his reaction to the words he was speaking. He could see no signs at all which gave him any indication as to how his story was being perceived; it was as if he was looking at a blank wall, hesitantly he continued. "She told me the family story concerned a great treasure discovered on the sea shore by one of her ancestors, but it was also said if it was ever revealed to anyone, the secret it contained was so powerful and the hoard so great, it would lead to the death of the entire family, so it must be kept a secret for ever. Grace told me how the tale of the treasure was next to useless as it was something held in trust but could never be used. It was called in the family "The curse of the Wrights." Well Master Hopkins, now you know what I know," concluded Thomas.

"Yes indeed Thomas, now I know what you know, and that of course is next to nothing. Your tale can be heard a thousand times a year in ale houses across the land," sneered Hopkins, rapidly tiring of this stupidity. "If the treasure had been in the family for so long and was as large as you say, surely after all this time someone would have retrieved it and spent it."

"Yes sir, you would think so, but the story also tells of many searches for it over the centuries by not only the King's men but by nobles and men of substance, as well as rapscallions and fortune seekers. Each time the search has come close to either Lynn or the Wright family, people have died. If it were just a few gold coins, I'm sure the original finder would have spent them all instead of hiding them and telling future generations of the dangers which surround its discovery, a danger for all concerned."

"So if your pillow talk unearthed this tale Thomas, why have you never tried to find it yourself, you seem to be an able enough fellow to know what to do on its discovery," mocked Matthew cocking his head to his right.

"Well Master Hopkins, I tried to wheedle more information about its hiding place from Grace over the years, but each time the subject came up, she refused to discuss it with me and was terrified someone else might overhear our conversation. She was convinced if anyone got wind of the tale; it would lead to the destruction of her and all her loved ones, including me. After a while we just did not mention it and after a further while, it went out of my head completely and then of course I met Emma Godfrey and the last thing on my mind was an old story of a family curse."

Matthew pondered the narrative and told Thomas he would think on his words. He then turned on his heel and opened the door to the cell and disappeared, leaving Thomas alone in the gloom of his lonely prison. Thomas Dempster flopped down onto the straw on his cell floor, knowing he had gambled his last and only item of any value with the man who would shortly seal his fate along with those of Grace and Emma. Thomas thought about the words he had spoken and the responses given by the Witchfinder and knew he could not have said any more to convince him of the truth of his story. Thomas sat for hours dissecting each moment of their discourse. He even reversed the roles of the two men in his mind and asked himself if he would act on such a wild story, he came to the inescapable conclusion he would not. So why therefore, should he be believed by the notorious Matthew Hopkins, a man with wealth, status and great power.

Only time would reveal all.

Chapter Five

Matthew had a sleepless night which left him agitated at breakfast. He was irritable with both the fawning landlord, who was as ever trying to please his valued guests and he was sharp with John Stearne. Dempster's words had tumbled and twisted in his head all night. Although he had received numerous bribes or promises of family help or wealth in return for the freedom of a loved one, this story was somehow different. It was too vague, it suggested things rather than stated them, it hinted at prospects both fair and foul. He realised Thomas Dempster had told him the tale as a last ditch attempt at saving his neck, but if it was Matthew in the same position, he was sure he would have come up with a far more enticing story than the one he had heard yesterday afternoon. Matthew was also impressed by the way Dempster had used the word "trust." He appeared to take the view whatever the outcome of the forthcoming trial may be it would be the hand of God and not the hand of Hopkins, Corbett or Robinson which would finally seal the fate of his future. This made him feel absolved from the responsibility of this man's life and this was a feeling new to him. Usually the burden of responsibility was a cross he felt he had to bear. People had no idea how traumatic performing God's will could be. He could not help himself but he knew instinctively he liked the labourer. There was something about the man.

Indeed, he spoke in a way unusual for a man of his station and he certainly had an air of command about him. Matthew thought how in this time of war, Thomas would make a great soldier for the army of Parliament and knew it was a shame the man's obvious talents had not been recognised. Dempster had wasted a productive life, hidden here in the depths of Kings Lynn. It was then Matthew resolved to speak to Grace Wright and see what she might have to say about the subject. Who knows what the morrow might bring.

His day brightened immediately upon his decision and he shared a joke with the landlord who came to ask him if his morning repast was sufficient. With a lighter step, he and John Stearne walked the couple of hundred yards through the filling streets of Lynn, now bustling with people about their daily work. Most people they passed tipped their hats or stood to one side as the two guests of the town made their way to return to their civic duties at the Trinity Guildhall. John and Matthew enjoyed this deference to their notoriety and it always amazed them how well known and admired they were across the land, or maybe the deference was in fact easier to explain, probably they were just feared. Either way it did not bother the two men. On the walk, it was decided Matthew would speak to both Cecily Taylor and Katherine Banks and John would take Dorothy Griffin and Thomasine Parker.

Matthew interviewed both his prisoners speedily yet thoroughly, concluding both were guilty, but his mind was on other things, both women denied their guilt but independently both implicated each other and Dorothy Lee. After his meeting with Lee yesterday, these two witness statements ensured she would

MATTHEW AND THE KILDERKIN

hang as a witch. The watchers of both Taylor and Banks had observed nothing, but the goodwife assigned to them had heard Taylor speaking in her sleep. She was prepared to testify she had not only heard her speaking to the Devil in tongues but whilst asleep a low moaning, as if the Devil was fornicating with her, came from her mouth. It had been a good morning's work and John and he were making the sort of progress with the prisoners the stalwart and upright citizens of Lynn would approve of.

Matthew and John took lunch with the Mayor of Lynn, Edward Robinson and Miles Corbett, the Recorder. They were joined by the vicar of St Margaret's, John Almond. Almond waxed lyrical about his church, with its history dating back to 1101 and the wonderful brasses from the 1360's showing Robert Braunche and his two wives, Letitia and Margaret. Matthew had met John Almond the previous night whilst using the church in prayer. Stearne was obviously disinterested at this new turn in the conversation and started to engage in conversation with Miles Corbett, who was sat at his side. Matthew soon got bored and wished the man Almond, would stop talking about the history of his church, but he and the Mayor, both appeared outwardly courteous and polite and listened with apparent interest at his historical ramblings. Robert Braunche was an important man in the 1360's as he was not only a rich, successful and powerful local merchant but had also been the Lord Mayor of Lynn, so Edward Robinson listened intently about tales of his predecessor. The lunch was fine but the conversation seemed interminable.

Edward interrupted the vicar to tell Matthew that one of the vicar's cherished brasses, depicted what had become known as the Peacock Feast, a feast which was held in honour of a visit to Lynn by King Edward III, of course in those days the town was known as Bishop's Lynn.

"What brought The King of England to Lynn?" asked Matthew casually.

"Well Master Hopkins, legend has it he was looking for something," smiled John Almond, glad that he was being quizzed about the history of his church and the town, two subjects upon which he prided himself. He was always happy to share his knowledge with people. "I think he was after a fine young buxom Norfolk girl to take home as a bed warmer," said the vicar winking at Edward, both men laughed at this risqué riposte.

"There are many local tales as to why he came here Matthew; they range from looking for a country estate, to finding another mad wife for his son, The Black Prince. The theories also encompassed theories about him looking for gold to one of searching for sites to enable him to establish a new port on the East coast," responded Edward, who was concentrating more on cutting another piece of ham from the joint than on his tale.

"Gold Edward?" asked Matthew raising a curious eyebrow.

"Yes," said the Mayor, stuffing the slice of ham into his mouth and chewing vigorously, "there are many local tales of lost treasure, all stuff and nonsense you know," said Edward motioning to the landlord with his knife to refill his tankard.

"Well they have to be somewhere Edward," said the vicar in a matter of fact way while eyeing up the soused sausages which lay before him.

"What has to be somewhere?" asked Matthew leaning a little closer to the vicar and now paying more attention to the man's wittering's.

MATTHEW AND THE KILDERKIN

"Why, the Crown Jewels of course!" he exclaimed in surprise, looking at his guest as if he were an idiot. "The very Crown Jewels which King John lost in the Wash in 1215 of course!" retorted John Almond.

Matthew felt an involuntary shiver run down his spine as he heard these words. He felt his cheeks tingle.

No it couldn't be.

Impossible: Out of the question.

He felt his face slowly drain of colour as a multitude of thoughts and possibilities ran Pell Mell through his head.

"Are you OK Matthew?" asked John Stearne, leaning towards his companion, concern showing in his voice. John had noticed his friend's sudden change of pallor.

"Yes I'm fine thank you John. I was just thinking of the enormous task ahead of us, trying to find the myriad of demons lurking throughout the land," said Matthew quietly, his thoughts far away.

"I'll drink to that," said Edward, raising his tankard in a salutary gesture. The other three men clanked their pewter ware together and John Almond, vicar of St Margaret's wiped his mouth on his sleeve and said, "To God's work."

Matthew sipped his drink and muttered to himself, "To God's work indeed."

Chapter Six

Hopkins and Stearne conscientiously returned to their task in the vaults beneath the Trinity Guildhall leaving the others to enjoy whatever delights the landlord could provide to enhance their afternoon.

It had been agreed their tasks were nearing completion, all the prisoners had been spoken to and most appeared to be guilty of the charges brought before them and the two men thought the evidential case against most of them was already sufficient to ensure convictions. Matthew told John he would speak to both Grace Wright and once again to Thomas Dempster. John Stearne would talk to Cecily Taylor and Katherine Banks the two women Matthew had seen that morning.

Matthew sat down at his makeshift table in his cell and thought for a long while, head bowed and chin resting on his entwined fists. Finally arousing himself from his contemplative mood he adjusted the light from his lantern as he started to review the notes he had already made about the people he had interviewed, adding extra thoughts as they occurred to him. His concentration was slipping and he found his mind kept drifting to the story of lost treasure he had heard over lunch and then to the story related to him by Thomas Dempster. He pushed his papers to one side and placed his elbows on the table in front of him and with both hands cradled his head, covering his eyes with his palms as he tried to block out the other sounds of voices he could hear drifting along the passageway from the other cells. He must think. Could there be a connection? Ten minutes of solitude passed and then he called out for the gaoler and instructed Grace Wright to be brought to him. She appeared a short while later, legs shackled and she was led into the room by the goodwife and the gaoler. The gaoler took her roughly by the shoulders and forced her down onto the chair. She exhibited no signs of emotion or resistance. Grace Wright looked every inch a desperate woman. Head bowed low with a posture which showed utter desolation and defeat. After Matthew had spent a moment or two mentally summing up the Wright woman, he asked the goodwife and the gaoler to leave them alone. The gaoler obediently turned to leave the room but the goodwife muttered how the request was unusual and she should stay if he was talking to a female prisoner, after all Wright's statements to Master Hopkins would need to be witnessed and corroborated

Matthew heard her and rounded on the poor woman asking her how on earth she would know what was usual or unusual in these circumstances, how many witches had she ever confronted, did she know their ruses, was she aware how the demons sometimes had to be either tricked out or cajoled into revealing their presence. What were her qualifications to judge such a matter? Under whose edict was she working? Who had summoned her here on behalf of the town? Before this diatribe from the Witchfinder, the goodwife visibly blanched and licked her rapidly drying lips. The haranguing continued unabated, "If you wish to take charge and carry on with this investigation, I will have no objections, I will simply tell Master Corbett and The Lord Mayor they need not have employed my services or expertise at great cost to the town as they already have an experienced witchfinder here in Lynn, in the shape of your good-self," fumed Hopkins to the poor woman. He stopped his rant and looked her unblinkingly in the eye, daring her to usurp him again.

"I meant no harm by it Master Hopkins, I'm sorry to have spoken out of turn sir," she said, as she hurried from the room, closing the door as she left, terrified he might tell Miles Corbett of her remarks.

Matthew smiled to himself and turned to face Grace Wright.

"Mistress Wright, you have been accused of witchcraft by your peers here in the town of Lynn. You have been observed by your gaoler and your watchers, all made up of good, honest and true folk from the town and the country around. You have been interviewed by John Stearne. I can see evidence of the marks of his pricker upon your body; I also know Master Stearne found some of the Devils symbols on your person. All these people and the facts they have uncovered have led us to the same ultimate conclusion." Matthew lowered his eyes and solemnly made the sign of the cross as he continued. His voice had become grave, level and even. "Through your words, deeds and actions you are undoubtedly guilty, and will hang. My talking to you now is a mere formality, as will be the trial next month, as will be your death, as will be your burial, as will be your existence. Within a short while your memory will vanish from people's minds. There will be no reprieve for you, no one to speak on your behalf, no mercy, just this prison until your slow release into the hands of the Devil. Then the rope will crack taught around your throat and choke your last breath from your jerking, blackened faced body. Mistress Wright, I am not a sage or a seer, but in this, I can accurately predict the future. It is as sure as the sun will rise in the morning or that winter will follow autumn." Matthew sat at the table before Grace and noticed urine was streaming freely down her legs.

"There is no one to help you. Only one person in all these proceedings has spoken up for you, one Thomas Dempster." Upon hearing this name, Grace Wright raised her eyes to look into Matthews face. A faint momentary flicker of hope spread across them. Someone was thinking of her. Thomas, the man she had always loved was thinking of her.

"Thomas is a good man Master Hopkins." Grace said simply in a quiet but shaky voice. "I wish him well and must tell you, he is as innocent of these charges as I am." Grace instinctively knew the man in front of her would not believe her, this was to be her death knell. Even though she was a prisoner whose fate was sealed, she silently despised everything he stood for. Tales of his cruelty, arrogance, coldness and greed, coupled with the fear he put into the communities he visited had travelled around with him, now it was her turn to face this living demon here on earth. She knew, even at this late stage he could still make her remaining few weeks of life a living hell on earth, so she kept all her thoughts to herself. Too many rumours about prisoners who had given vent to their spleen directly to his face and the dire consequences which befell them had been told. Keeping her dignity and counsel was more important to Grace.

"You have been adjudged to be guilty of your crimes and the law will take its course, only the sentencing remains and we both know what that will prove to be." Matthew said evenly. "Grace, there is only one person on God's green earth who can help you in your current position," he said leaning closer to the woman sat before him and then lowering his voice he continued. "That one person is me. Grace, I would go to my grave with a heavy heart if I did not give every accused person the opportunity of redemption in God's eyes, if I thought the saving of even one soul might be possible, I would hold my hand out to help. Take note and hark well, I am about to give you one last, final, chance. Do you fully understand my words to you Mistress Wright? Do you trust me enough to help me enable your own redemption and salvation?" He spoke slowly and with great deliberation. He then straightened himself in his chair and fixed her eyes with a piercing stare while clasping his hands in front of him, as if in prayer. He waited a minute or two in complete silence. The air between the two of them hung still, heavily and solid.

Matthew then continued, he had resolved to ask this question of Grace Wright once only and then put an end to all this nonsense. "Thomas Dempster said you had told him your family had been afflicted for generations and how you spoke to him of the curse of the Wrights. If I can prove to my satisfaction this curse is a reality, I can and will use my powers of advocacy to speak on your behalf at your forthcoming trial. I will then know if such a spell truly exists, you and your forefathers may have been bewitched by demons stretching back across the years and it might be argued you had no control over your current path as your destiny has been pre-ordained and as such you must be innocent. Proving the family curse is not a lie will enable me to lift it from your shoulders and those of Thomas Dempster, who has also become infected by the knowledge of its very existence. In Gods eyes you will then be untainted and salvation could be yours. If the curse cannot be proven, you will both surely hang, guilty as charged after the next sessions."

Grace sat before the most feared man in England and realised as much as she hated this abomination of a man, this was indeed her final and only chance of prolonging her life. It lifted her heart when she realised that Thomas Dempster might still love her. Her wonderful, precious Thomas had been trying to save her life, even at this late stage in the proceedings. This must be proof of how he still loved her. Her heart skipped at the thought of him having interceded on her behalf with the foul Hopkins, this cruel and malicious Witchfinder. She had always known deep within how her Thomas would tire of his whore Emma Godfrey and one day realise she, Grace Wright was the only one who truly loved him. Grace had always known he would come back to her one day and then they would be together for all eternity. Her arms and heart had always been open for him. This was her chance to be with the man she loved. She resolved instantly she would do whatever the Witchfinder asked of her to ensure her future with Thomas Dempster, her Thomas.

She raised her head and spoke, "Yes sir, the Wrights have carried a curse for hundreds of years," she said, keeping her eyes lowered in case he should see anything in them he disliked or disapproved of. "What do you wish to know of me Master Hopkins?"

Matthew knew that while alone with Grace, he could ask of her what he desired, as there was no one to confirm any possible allegations which may be made in the future by the prisoner, not that anyone would believe the words of a convicted witch, fighting for her life, against Matthew Hopkins, Witchfinder. Furthermore, he had no desire to let anyone else know of the content of the imminent conversation. "I know you have made claim as to your family being put under a curse for many years, I would like to know

MATTHEW AND THE KILDERKIN 61

what the curse is and why the Wrights have been subjected to it and of course, who made it," replied Matthew.

Grace sat before him feeling degraded as the puddle of urine she was sat in cooled on her bottom and thighs and she was acutely conscious of her demeaning circumstances. She felt as wretched and guilty as she had done when her father had caught her stealing apples when she was seven. "Well sir, it happened many years ago, some questions I can answer and some I cannot. I can only vow to tell you the truth of what I know. The tale was told to me by my father and recounted to him by his father. This has been the case since anyone can remember. It is a very quick and simple tale to report. It is said within the family how a great treasure was found, one which has brought ill luck and bad fortune to all who speak of it or who try and retrieve it from its resting place. Death has stalked all who talk of its very existence." Grace told Matthew.

"Go on, tell me more. Where did this treasure come from, what sort of things have happened, how are you cursed and by whom?"

Grace lifted her eyes and looked at the witch-hunter, then continued, "The treasure is supposed to be the Crown Jewels sir, both they and other things, of which I know nothing, were found by an ancestor of mine, William Wright, on the mud banks of the estuary. King John lost them in the cold grey waters and it is said how he was cursed for doing so by God himself, along with any whoever saw them again. King John died horribly, as God's punishment for having lost them. The Crown Jewels are really God's jewels sir, and are worn to show the King of Heaven has invested his power in the King here on earth, a holy symbol."

Matthew was excited by the story pouring from Grace Wright's lips. Up until now it had all sounded feasible and although he could not agree with the blasphemy that his sweet God could curse anyone, he let her continue.

"When King John lost them, God was angry and struck him down dead. Well, his rule was followed by Good King Henry and it is said he spent all of his reign searching in vain for them. Everyone knew the Crown Jewels were lost in the dark waters of the Wash, but King Henry and the local people all knew the tides would probably, eventually return them somewhere to the shore. The King had put spies in all of the towns surrounding the Wash, listening out for rumours or tales of people with newly found wealth. Many people went missing during his reign sir, there were many unexplained bodies found floating in the waters of the Wash and lying out on the Fens. It is said he reigned for fifty odd years and never forgot about the treasure in all that time, always keeping a wary eye on Lynn and the surrounding towns and their peoples. When King Henry died, the new King, Edward, must have lost interest in the story of the lost Crown Jewels, it seems Old Longshanks had more to worry him than some old tale of treasure lost in the Norfolk mud. They say in the Wright family how eleven members were tortured or went missing during King Henry's reign. He was determined to find what King John had lost. The treasure had been hidden by my ancestor William Wright, who had found it, and none dared disturb it for fear not only for their own lives but for the lives of everyone they knew. Master Hopkins sir, if God's curse on the jewels had already killed one King and many people from these parts as well as members of my own family, it shows me it is not a wise thing to hunt for, let alone to have discovered." Grace continued, "Anyway, if a Wright did dig them up and try to sell them, who in their right minds would want to buy the Crown Jewels? Everyone would soon know what it was and who had dug it up and all knew who the rightful owner was. No one could keep a secret like that. Sir, it would spell death and disaster for all concerned when the King of England discovered the treasure was no longer beneath the mud of the Wash. Imagine the retribution which would rain down when he discovered it was being hidden by the Wright family, poor folk from Norfolk. People who were now touting it around and trying to sell it, like a purse snatched from a town market. The family say how we might be rich but can't spend any of it, ever. My father reckoned it was all rubbish anyhow, but he had been made to promise, like his father before him, he would pass on the tale. Now Master Hopkins, I have passed it on to you."

Grace sat silently, her eyes cast down to the floor.

"An interesting tale Mistress Wright, but I have heard similar ones many times before, the problem with this one, as with many others, is that it has no weight and cannot be proven. I am unable to establish that you find yourself in your current state of affairs because of a curse which may have been placed on your family at some time in the ancient past. I have no way of knowing the curse truly exists because I have no way of knowing if the items which you say have brought the curse down upon you and yours even exist!" Matthew responded in clear measured tones, hoping if she knew of the location of any treasure, this might tip the balance in ascertaining its current location. He rose from his chair saying, "So you see my predicament Mistress Wright, unless you can demonstrate the items you mention actually exist, I can never prove such a curse exists. This means neither Thomas Dempster nor myself can prove your innocence or help you any further."

"Master Hopkins, I am telling you the truth, I can't see how I can prove my story unless you are willing to help me and retrieve the treasure to see for yourself that it is the honest truth I speak!"

Grace sobbed, and rubbed her running nose on her sleeve, realising her final chance at happiness with Thomas was slipping inexorably from her grasp.

"You expect me to dig holes all over Norfolk on the off chance you might be telling me the truth? Even if you are not lying and I do find the Crown Jewels, you then expect me and my family to become cursed in the same way you claim your family has been cursed for hundreds of years? You ask too much of me Mistress Wright!" exclaimed Matthew.

"But sir, you are the only hope I have of proving my innocence. Master Hopkins, fear not, you will not have to dig holes all over Norfolk, I am able to tell you the exact spot where the curse of the Wrights is hidden. Surely sir, your family will not be damned by God as it will be a righteous thing which you will be doing in his eyes, lifting the curse from me and mine and freeing my soul to soar to heaven at the appointed time. Surely God can only be grateful to you for restoring to him what is rightfully his, both my soul and his Crown Jewels."

Matthew turned away from Grace and smiled wryly; he had come to the point he had hoped to reach with the woman more quickly and far easier than he had anticipated. Matthew knew he had nothing to lose, if he could restore the treasure to its rightful owners, Oliver Cromwell and the people of the commonwealth, he would become rich beyond measure and the money would secure not only his position but that of his family for many generations to come. He would become a prominent national hero combined with becoming a new man of substance. If she was lying, he had only lost an hour or two of his time and she would still hang, along with Dempster and the rest of the vermin here in Lynn. It would also be a salutary lesson to his vanity and pride how even he could have been tricked by one of her Devils. This would surely help him in his future work, knowing yet another impish ploy to look out for and be on his guard against.

"Mistress Wright, I tire of this unseemly banter and your shallow lies, I bid you good day and will see you for the last time at your trial," said Matthew with his back still towards Grace and moving towards the door.

"On the south tower of St Margaret's church there is a sign on the wall, it is near that mark." Grace blurted out quickly, realising her only chance of survival and future happiness was just about to leave her life forever. "When you find the sign, you walk to the right, along the building for exactly twenty six feet from the marked point and it lies buried below, just one yard out from the wall."

Matthew stopped dead in his tracks, still facing the door, with his back to Grace; this had been his final ploy in getting her to tell him of its whereabouts. He surmised that if she knew the location, she would tell him or if she was lying, he would simply walk away from her life. He remained motionless and still with his back to his prisoner he asked softly, his mind was now focussed and alert. "What sort of a sign?"

"It is a cross etched in to the stonework sir. That is the point from which you start. Follow the directions I have given you and you will find the curse is buried below in an old oak barrel." Grace's eyes bored into the witch-hunters back, she was biting her lip and silently praying he would turn around. Please turn around.

The Witchfinder stood erect and said, "If you have told me the truth, salvation may yet be yours Grace Wright, salvation for you and your lover Thomas Dempster." With that, without looking at Grace Wright, Hopkins left the room.

As the gaoler took her back to her cell, she hoped the story of the curse of the Wrights and the location of the treasure which had been handed down for generation on generation had not been an old wives tale but was indeed as truthful as her father had sworn to her.

Now all she could do was to wait and pray. Hoping the abhorrent Witchfinder creature would find what he was seeking, which would ensure not only her own freedom and safety but also of her beloved Thomas.

Chapter Seven

Matthew returned quickly to the Inn and went to his room to think on the tale he had just been told. He knew her story had now left him no choice, he had to investigate further. He was convinced Grace had only told him the story, knowing this to be her last chance of life. If as he secretly hoped, the curse of the Wrights turned out to be the lost Crown Jewels of King John and he could retrieve them intact, then what next? He was excited, but this had to be thoroughly considered.

Matthew concluded he must not let anyone know of the find, if word got to a Royalist sympathizer, and there were still many about, even here in Norfolk, his life would be in mortal danger. There would be many amongst them who would take the jewels from Matthew, probably killing him in the process, to give them to King Charles to enable him to once and for all turn the tide of this war against the people of England and the army of Parliament. Rumours were rife and he had recently heard tales of the King fleeing Oxford. His son Charles, Prince of Wales, one day to be Charles II, rumoured to be on the Island of Jersey, would surely use them as a rallying point for the start of raising an army for an invasion. So many damnable rumours were flying through the air around him. No, the Crown Jewels must be kept from the hands of the Royalists at all costs.

Some years earlier, Matthew had gained an interest in the Thorn Inn at Mistley a place he loved. It was easily accessible along a riverside path from his home in neighbouring Manningtree. It was said by some of the older inhabitants of the village how they could remember waving at ships leaving to fight the Spanish Armada. He now used the Inn as his second home. It also acted as a base from which he could embrace his practices. The Thorn Inn was widely known around the east of the country and it was to here many came to inform against witches they thought might be lurking within their own communities. It was also here where he received visits from many famous persons and in so doing increased his influence on some of the countries most celebrated people and upon its political elite. Matthew rejoiced in the position he held and always knew he was destined for greatness and was now acutely aware he was beginning to fulfil his destiny. His mother and father would swell with pride if they could now see the person he was striving hard to become.

William Lilly was one of the many people of influence who had stayed with Matthew at the Thorn Inn and was now the country's leading and most influential astrologer. Matthew knew William had contacts on both sides of the political divide as well as with prominent members of the country's aristocracy. His works were extensive and he was well read. Matthew realised that he could use William to sound out any knowledge of the jewels if rumours surfaced, as he not only had an ear in both the Royalist and Parliamentarian camps, but would also be able to tell from his astrological divinations. Why, even Matthew had consulted with William on various matters pertaining to shipping and their

MATTHEW AND THE KILDERKIN

cargoes, when he had been a shipping agent, before he had turned to the law and had taken up his quest to rid the country of its demons. He still had an interest in shipping matters. He also found this an easy way to begin conversations with William before asking questions and receiving instruction about the darker aspects of the "Signs of the Times" appertaining to witchcraft and other practices upon which William, using his God given gift could enlighten him. William told Matthew the story of how he once used divining rods made of hazel to hunt for treasure in the cloisters of Westminster Abbey. On that occasion the rods crossed over each other and the spectators present ordered the labourers, who accompanied the party, to dig down at that point. The men discovered no treasure, but instead a body in a coffin. It was also on that evening when a terrible blustering wind blew up threatening to demolish the west end of the Abbey. William managed to dismiss the demons causing this. William and Matthew had lots in common.

John Thurloe was another regular caller to see Matthew at the Inn and he was always greeted with friendship and warmth. John and Matthew had much in common; they were both the sons of clergymen. John was the son of Thomas Thurloe, the rector of Abbess Roding in Essex. While Matthew's father James was vicar at Great Wenham in Suffolk, until he sadly died a dozen or so years ago. Both John and Matthew were about the same age and they had both studied law as young men, through which profession they made their first acquaintance. Since then, John had become heavily involved in the closeted world of Oliver Cromwell and his coterie, being appointed as one of the Secretaries to the Commissioners of Parliament at the Treaty of Uxbridge. John was not only one of Matthew's oldest and closest friends, but he was a direct link to many other Government sources in London. Matthew decided he must meet with John, but before he could do so, he must make other plans. If of course the treasure proved to be a reality!

Earlier, Matthew had casually told the landlord he would take a walk around the town before joining John Stearne for supper. Matthew had only one destination in mind. The stroll through the emptying streets of Kings Lynn was brisk and purposeful. People were making their way home to join their families. Matthew went into St Margaret's to pray, marvelling at not only the brasses which had made the vicar, John Almond so animated but at the intricate carving of the great oak pews. Many people passed through the doors and the evening's sermon was well attended. After people had left he had a pleasant talk with John Almond. After a while Almond made his own excuses and left. Matthew found himself alone. When he had finished his devotions he left through the west door, nestled between the two soaring towers and rounded the church to the much lower southern tower. Matthew stood alone. There was no one else about. He was now concentrating on the wall to his left, carefully inspecting it as he walked slowly backwards and forwards. He was trying to spot any undulations in the wall cast by the rapidly setting sun. He must have made a strange sight to anyone glancing at him as they hurried by, but the Witchfinder had his head bowed as he looked down at the stonework and believed if anyone recognised him, they would presume he was in a state of prayer, contemplating the fate of others as he took the evening air. He thought if anyone were to identify him, they would feel saddened, assuming he was at prayer, trying to resolve the burden of responsibility for the souls of others which must weigh heavily upon his shoulders. Then something caught his eye making him stop, a vague shape, much lower than he had anticipated, probably only a foot above the ground and partially obscured by the weeds and grass growing against the wall. Kneeling down he gently parted the greenery and he could definitely make out the sign of an engraved cross, obviously ancient and well weathered, but nonetheless, there it was, as Grace Wright had said it would be. It then dawned on him he may be kneeling near the lost Crown Jewels of England. Jewels lost by King John, in the year 1216, four hundred and thirty years previously. Matthew looked towards the heavens and uttered a silent prayer and smiled to himself. Looking surreptitiously around the area he was convinced he was alone and no one was looking at him, no matter how innocently. He carefully paced twenty six feet and pressed his heel into the grass. He returned to the cross and paced out this distance three times more and each time his heel mark was under his foot. He must have made a strange sight to anyone looking. Then he studied his surroundings yet again and made sure no one was observing his actions, you can't be too careful he mused to himself as he paced one full yard from the wall and stuck his knife into the ground making a small mark, but one which he was sure he could identify later. On the south side of the church, there were no houses or roads but if four hundred and thirty years ago, William Wright had picked the area by the northern tower to bury his treasure, this would now be in full view of everyone who used the centre of the town, making retrieval impossible without arousing far too many questions. The north tower was built on the side which now contained the market place, a place where Grace Wright was now certain to hang.

At supper later that evening, John Stearne and Matthew agreed their work in Lynn was all but complete and decided they would return to their homes for a while until the trial began here in Lynn. This should be sometime towards the end of September. Matthew hoped this would give him the time he required to set his plan in motion.

The next morning Matthew rose early and left the Inn, making several arrangements before returning to join John Stearne, Mayor Robinson and the Recorder, Miles Corbett for breakfast. It was determined both Matthew and John would return to Lynn later next month with their prepared cases against the nine witches, who would still be languishing beneath the Trinity Guildhall awaiting their trial and futures The trial date was set at September 24th. Now came the tricky bit, the payment of the fee for his and Stearne's services. This was always an embarrassing moment for Matthew. The monies to be paid had not been set beforehand, but all around the table knew Matthew and John had been summoned to Lynn at the request of the town and the fee could not be too modest as a result. Mayor Robinson told Matthew it had been decided the fee payable was to be one of fifteen pounds for duties deemed to have been exceptionally well performed. For once Matthew was shocked into silence, all of his prepared arguments about the level of the amount were not needed. Matthew had not expected to have been offered anywhere near this sum for such a straight forward use of his time. He was inwardly delighted and looked across the table and saw John Stearne smile and gave him a conspiratorial wink. In their wildest dreams they had hoped for a fee of ten pounds, but fifteen. Well, maybe the world was going mad. This now meant both men could have a timely break with their friends and family with a pocket full of money to take home from their toils. It is said the Devil looks after his own, Matthew was not too sure about that but knew God certainly did.

It was further agreed by Robinson and Corbett, a second fee of two pounds would be paid for Matthew's testimony during the

MATTHEW AND THE KILDERKIN

forthcoming September sessions of the peace. Mayor Robinson and Miles Corbett gave thanks on behalf of the townsfolk of Kings Lynn to the two men, then gave their apologies and left the Inn to attend upon civic business. Matthew and John both smiled at each other and reached across the table to shake hands as the men left. This happens often in towns they visit, they are welcomed when they arrive, but when their task is complete, the people of the town want them to leave as quickly and with as little fuss as possible. This was predictable and did not bother either the Witchfinder or his colleague.

"I will be leaving in a short while Matthew," said a still smiling Stearne. "Will you ride with me for a while until our roads part?"

"I'm afraid not John," said Matthew, taking five pounds from his fee and giving them to John, "I have had my eye on some fine tables I wish to buy for the Inn and have made arrangements for their purchase and for a carter to take them to Mistley, I will accompany him. It will be some company for me on the trip home. The next time John Stearne eats with Matthew Hopkins at the Thorn Inn it will be from a handsomely carved table from Lynn!" Both men smiled at the prospect.

"I will send you a message when I next need you John. May God be with you on your own journey, I wish your wife well," said Matthew rising and giving his companion a bear like hug.

"God speed Matthew," said Stearne as he turned and left the Inn.

Matthew awoke early and met John Almond at his church. Matthew told the vicar how he was leaving Lynn early the next morning and how he had bought some furniture for his Inn at Mistley, but he had nowhere to store it overnight. Matthew asked if he could store it in the church. John Almond said it would be his pleasure to help Matthew in such a small way after the service he had done for the town by rooting out the presence of witches in Lynn. They were an abomination within the community and he swore he would ceaselessly work for their discovery in Matthew's absence. Matthew smiled broadly saying, "While there are good and enlightened men like you walking this earth, how can we not rid our countryside of this plague." At these words of endorsement and encouragement from none other than Matthew Hopkins, John Almond visibly straightened and beamed.

"Master Hopkins, I will make sure one of my parishioners stays with your possessions over night to ensure their safety." Matthew was delighted, not only had he secured a safe place overnight, but his very own guard!

It was a simple task to have the few sticks of furniture and the few tools he had purchased, placed in the church. He spent a little time arranging for the services of the carter, now he felt ready to complete his plan. At dusk, Matthew returned to the wall under the south tower and immediately found the etched cross. It took him seconds to find the gouge in the grass he had made earlier with the knife. After looking to make sure he was not being observed and giving a silent prayer that his journey to Lynn may prove to be even more profitable than it had already been, he firmly pushed the spade he had brought with him from the Inn into the hard earth. Matthew had no idea how deep the barrel or chest which contained the curse of the Wrights may be hidden, but never did he expect to reveal wood after turning his first sod. Matthew stopped and looked down and then cleared some loose soil with his hand, yes, it was a wooden object. He furtively looked around once more, his paranoia rising. All was clear. His heart was pounding in his chest as he turned more earthen sods in rapid succession and quickly revealed the circular top of a barrel. It lay less than a foot beneath the surface. He had revealed a circle of oak about 18 inches in diameter. Matthew guessed this to be a kilderkin barrel. He had seen many of these in his own Inn. He carried on digging and after fifteen minutes he had exposed a barrel about two feet long and about twenty inches diameter at its middle. He was absolutely positive he had not been seen by a mortal soul. This was far too easy. God must be approving of his work. He knelt and grasped his arms around the barrel and rocked it backwards and forwards. The oak looked in excellent condition, but the ground did not want to give up its four hundred year old secret. Matthew returned to his digging, exposing more of the barrel until he knew there was no more remaining and then he knelt once more and rocked the kilderkin. He felt it move and heard a slurping noise and realised the sodden earth had released its captive. He was surprised at how light the barrel was. He had handled many a kilderkin at the Thorn Inn and knew it to usually contain sixteen gallons of ale, but thankfully, this was much lighter and he managed to pull it out of the hole he had made without expending too much energy. Matthew quickly re-filled the hole and realised when all the soil was replaced he was left with a deep impression caused by the removal of the kilderkin. There was nothing he could do about that now. He hoped no one would notice, but frankly, was unconcerned if they did. In the gathering gloom, Matthew looked around him once more and was heartened to see there was still no one in sight. After a closer inspection of the barrel, he found no breach in its oak surface. Although the metal hoops were very rusty, they were perfectly tight, all seemed wonderfully intact. Matthew realised the William Wright who had buried the barrel in the thirteenth century must have been a wright by trade and although he probably dealt with wheels, Matthew guessed he was also a very competent cooper and had made a barrel of the finest oak and to the most exacting of standards, but Matthew believed even William Wright would never have expected his handiwork to have been admired after four hundred years buried in the ground. Yet, here it was, on the grass before his eyes. So there really was a curse of the Wrights! Only time would tell what mysteries, surprises or disappointments the cask contained. Matthew carried the spade jauntily over his shoulder as he kick-rolled the kilderkin around the side of the church and banged on the main door. The guard appointed by John Almond cautiously opened the door a crack. When he saw the Witchfinder standing before him, he opened the door wide and said, "Master Hopkins sir, come in, come in sir. No one has been here to disturb your furniture or belongings sir," he volunteered as he half bowed while he raised his hand to touch his forelock. Matthew smiled to the man as he saw his possessions all still neatly stored in the wide space in front of the font.

"Here are some more additions to my belongings to take home to Mistley on the morrow," said Matthew, trying hard to contain his excitement now he knew for certain the barrel actually existed. I will be here early in the morning with the carter to start my journey, "I pray God grants you a peaceful night." As he uttered these words Matthew noticed the guard glance at the muddied kilderkin, then without a second thought he rolled it across the flagstone floor and stood it on end next to the rest of Matthew's belongings, finally resting the spade against it. Then he turned around and returned to Matthew's side to open the door for his famous guest. Matthew heard the great lock in the door turn amid many a "Goodnight sir" emanating from the other side of the now secured door. He walked back to the Inn for what he judged would be a fitful night's sleep.

He found a seat by the fire and took a comforting glass of wine, lost deep within his own thoughts as the business of the Inn bustled around him

Matthew arose early and had his final hearty breakfast served by a Landlord who was sorry to see his new friend leave his humble establishment. Now he felt prepared to start off on the first leg of his journey. Usually in a situation like this he would just let the carter make the delivery, but he thought on this occasion the goods being transported were far too valuable to be let out of his sight. Matthew knew deep down he would also be grateful for a little company on the eighty or so mile trip back to the Thorn Inn. His spirits were lifted when he was greeted by a jolly, ox like man in his fifties who introduced himself as Joseph. Matthew thought after his first meeting with Joseph he would prove to be far too enthusiastic and happy a man to make the journey with him, but Joseph the carter was recommended by John Almond and he assured Matthew he would make an agreeable companion for the trip. He was also a hardworking, honest and Christian soul who was a stalwart of John's own flock. In fact it was Joseph's brother who had remained vigilant and stood guard over Matthew's property during the night in St Margaret's church. Matthew watched as Joseph and his brother carefully loaded the goods onto the cart and made sure all was covered against the elements and secured with hemp ropes against the bumps and jerks which would be encountered along the roads. There was good natured, easy, light hearted banter between the two brothers and it became obvious from their conversation Joseph had never before made such a long journey. It also became apparent to Matthew how Joseph's business standing in the Kings Lynn area would multiply tenfold. Not only would he have undertaken work for the famous Matthew Hopkins, but he would have made a round journey of almost two hundred miles in the process! If he fulfilled this engagement to Master Hopkins satisfaction, this would reflect wonderfully on him and could give his business a much needed boost. Times were been hard since the infernal war had started between the King and the Parliament. Joseph was too old to fight, for which he constantly gave thanks to God, but had not been able to pick up any work from the army of Parliament and their garrisons around the area. All the garrisons required fodder for their mounts, powder, provisions, cloth, weapons, match, pike, and a thousand and one other items required to keep an army at the ready. Now maybe some of this work might just come his way. Matthew pondered his fee which had been agreed with Joseph and briefly thought he might have negotiated a smaller fee for the work, but soon dismissed the idea as he knew the fee agreed upon was fair to both men.

Matthew watched as Joseph set out on his journey south towards Mistley and saw the cart trundle its way along the rutted road from Lynn towards Thetford. He then returned to the Guildhall and announced he wished to see Thomas Dempster and Grace Wright once more before he left the town. Matthew was led once more down the few stairs to the lower level and along the dark passageway to Dempster's cell and was admitted, he turned to look at the gaoler, who took his cue and silently left the two men alone.

"Master Dempster, I trust you are in fine fettle this morning," asked Matthew.

"As well as a man in my position may be Master Hopkins," said Thomas, hoping the Witchfinder might give him some indication as to whether progress had been made in the case of the Wright curse. "Do you have any news for me sir?" asked Thomas.

"Master Dempster, I have spoken to the widow Wright and she told me there was indeed a family curse and how the tale went back many generations within her family. I have no way of knowing whether the curse is true or not. She cannot prove it one way or another and has no evidence which can possibly lead me to confirm it. Her story is just that, a story. She has certainly sentenced herself to death as a witch due to her own testimony and that of some others involved in her case."

Thomas's heart sank at this news. He had prayed the Witchfinder might believe Grace's story and hoped it would set him free to once again lie in the arms of Emma Godfrey. It did not now appear as if this would be likely to happen. "What will become of me Master Hopkins? I can only repeat I am innocent of all the charges levied upon me."

Matthew looked at the prisoner before him and said, "You have cavorted with a woman who is a known witch and will be found guilty as such, of that I have no doubt. This makes your position very delicate and you will probably be found guilty by association. I need to converse further with Master Stearne about you. You must hope that between now and the sessions in a few weeks' time, God intervenes on your behalf. I can do no more for you. Not at this time. I bid you good day Master Dempster." Matthew turned on his heel and left the cell, with just the noise of the door locking behind him. Thomas smiled silently to himself and wondered what the Witchfinder had meant by, "I can do no more for you. Not at this time," as he was considering these words it suddenly came to him that the sly bastard knew more than he was letting on. His heart raced and he felt almost elated. Maybe there was still a slight hope of freedom. Time would tell.

Matthew returned to the room where he had been holding his interviews and standing manacled before the desk was Grace Wright, he motioned to the goodwife to leave and this time she did so, immediately and without comment. "Widow Wright, I gave you one last chance yesterday, to recant your sins to me and tell me the truth. Instead I listened to your ridiculous story about a curse being handed down to your family via Kings. You linked yourself directly to both Kings and God in the same sentence. You spoke heresy and blasphemy. You told me a story so fantastic it is certain to hang you. I suppose the demons controlling your words told you that I, Matthew Hopkins, Witchfinder, man of God would be taken in by it. God does not curse Kings. God does not curse his subjects. God is not capable of such malfeasance. This is plainly the work of the Devil and all his demons which rise in hell and manifest themselves in the black hearts of men and women infected with the Devil's spawn." Matthew turned and left the room. He strode along the passageway and climbed the stairs, walking out of the Trinity Guildhall and into sunlight, breathing in the fresh morning air of King's Lynn, while a barrage of blasphemy, invocations, heresies, foul curses, swearing, shouting, hysteria, anger and madness echoed along the lonely empty passageway. A passage which would lead Grace Wright to her cell: then to her inevitable fate.

Matthew wasted no more time and walked briskly to the stables, mounted his saddled horse, turned his back on Lynn and spurred his mount south, towards Thetford. It took him less than an hour to catch up with Joseph and his precious cargo.

Matthew Hopkins had only to wait another couple of days and he could secrete himself in his rooms at the Thorn Inn and then he could safely reveal the secrets which William Wright's kilderkin had held secure for centuries. The Witchfinder knew at long last and with God's divine sanction, power, fame and fortune could soon be within his grasp.

Chapter Eight

It was summer 1647 and Matthew was travelling alone long the road from London back to Mistley, after meeting up with his old friend John Thurloe and Oliver Cromwell. Some called John, Oliver Cromwell's spy master and others referred to him as the number one Argus. His eyes were everywhere. Matthew knew of this reputation but to him he was just a good friend. The last few months had proven to be very eventful and nerve racking for Matthew. As he rode towards home through the Essex countryside, his mind recalled the sequence which had led him to this point. His thoughts returned to the events of mid-August 1646.

The journey from Lynn had proven uneventful as Matthew and his horse led the way for Joseph who studiously and carefully drove his cart along the sometimes desolate and lonely roads. Joseph had indeed proven to be good company on the long ride, passing the time amiably and casually with Matthew. Both men talked of many things to make the journey pass more speedily. They saw few other travellers outside of the precincts of the towns they journeyed through and Matthew guessed the closing stages of the war had taken most people away to other parts of the country. Matthew was greeted like a long lost friend when he arrived at the Thorn Inn in Mistley and everyone was glad to see him. The staff and customers were taken aback how he had gone to the trouble of bringing such wonderful furniture for their comfort and from so far away. This was uncharacteristically generous of the master. Joseph stayed for two nights as Matthew's guest before returning on his long journey. His mind and soul had been enriched by the conversation along the route with Matthew. He was still in awe of the fame of Master Hopkins, who seemed to be respected and recognised wherever they stopped. The folk he met in the Thorn at Mistley regaled him with stories from other shires and he was told of the latest news from the wars which seemed to be all but over, at long last. The Inn was busy and although Joseph knew little of the way in which commerce was conducted at an Inn, even he could see Matthew had a thriving business. He met many travellers, even one soldier who had been present when Kings Charles had surrendered to the Scots army at Newark earlier that year. Joseph also saw men who had just arrived from London and he listened in awe as they told him about the city and its people. He could not believe some of the tales of mighty churches, soldiers milling in the streets, the buildings and palaces, the shops, markets and the pace of life. It seemed from what he was told that everything was available and anything was possible; if you had the money. He knew upon his return to Lynn, he would be talk of the town amongst his social circle. Not only did he have the ear of Matthew Hopkins but he had also come away with the great man's heart-felt best wishes and of course with his money! He was now eager to return to Lynn, unsure whether he was feeling homesick or just wanted to get home to brag about his new status in life, either which-way Joseph left Mistley with a light heart and a zest and enthusiasm for his future.

Upon arriving home Matthew had the kilderkin taken to his rooms and attended to the business of the Inn for a day or so

MATTHEW AND THE KILDERKIN

making sure he aroused no suspicion on this all too brief return to Mistley. Matthew had given instructions not to be disturbed when in his own rooms, telling people he had papers and cases to prepare for several forthcoming sessions. He knew no one would dare disobey this request. Not only was he a man to be respected, but he was well and truly the master of his own home.

Eventually, after what had appeared to be a lifetime of anticipation he found himself alone, all business and necessary items regarding the Thorn Inn dealt with, people paid, orders placed, questions answered. He was certain he had not behaved in any unusual manner. It was only at that stage he felt relaxed enough to turn his full attention to the kilderkin. He had been dithering between ripping the kilderkin apart immediately on arrival or waiting, delaying the moment, when his overwhelming curiosity could be sated. He had decided to wait a while longer, not out of a need for self-flagellation but mainly in fear of the distress he would experience if the barrel did not conceal his future dreams. He needed to defray any moment of extreme disappointment, which in turn meant he put off the moment for as long as possible. He eyed the cask carefully and marvelled once more at the quality of the workmanship and could scarcely believe it had been made over four hundred years previously. He had opened many kilderkins over the years but he hoped this one might turn out to hold the most valuable wares in English history. He got to work on the barrel with the few tools he had secretly brought up to his bedroom during the course of the day. Although the barrel looked sturdy enough, in fact it was a very quick and easy task to remove the top end piece of the kilderkin. Immediately, an unfamiliar mustiness caught his nose as he removed the lid in its entirety. He found the barrel to be stuffed with what looked like sacking. Gently he began to remove the roughly woven cloth and as he did so he felt something weighty. The kilderkin had been lined with some sort of pitch or tar which had set solid and provided a watertight seal to protect the contents. He moved aside the cloth and noticed a golden glint catching the light. Matthew's heart skipped a beat. It was true. The curse of the Wrights was here on the table in front of him.

After five minutes or so, Matthew had carefully emptied the kilderkin and placed it on the floor by his chair and arranged its contents on a linen bed sheet which he had carefully spread over his desk. Now he could inspect his find at his leisure.

There were a dozen or so pieces which lay before him, all but one, golden and most bejewelled. There were four rings, two plain bands and two with mounted and clasped jewels, and a beautifully worked amulet. As if that were not enough there was also a silver orb which had become blackened and tarnished over the years and two magnificent crosses. These sat beside a Sceptre topped with a dove which glistened with stones of many colours. Matthew had heard of fine sapphires, diamonds, rubies and the like but had never seen anything resembling the size of the precious stones before him. He knew these alone were worth a King's ransom. The collection was completed by a golden Ampulla, the vessel which holds the oils used in the Coronation of Kings to anoint the head, breast and palms and of course the spoon which accompanies it. This was not quite the end of the kilderkin's secrets.

The biggest piece by far was a plain golden crown. This was obviously the fabled crown worn by Edward the Confessor at his Coronation. The famed King Edward crown! Matthew had seen in paintings of the canonised King wearing it. Matthew knew Edward's crown had been passed down to his successor in 1066.

MATTHEW AND THE KILDERKIN

The crown which sat before him had been worn by Saint Edward the Confessor, Harold Godwinson, William the Conqueror, William Rufus, Henry the First, King Steven, The Empress Matilda, King Henry the second and Richard the Lionheart. The Crown Jewels had finally adorned the head of Jean Sans Terre, John Lackland, King John, the man who had lost them for ever, consigned to the mud and waters of the Wash. That is until their miraculous recovery in 1646 by Matthew Hopkins. Matthew could not help himself but to give in to his own vanity, knowing any man responsible for the recovery of such an important national and international treasure as the Crown Jewels of England had earned, in fact deserved the right to place Edward's crown upon his own head. This he did. At once Matthew thought he could feel the ghosts of these great monarchs tumbling through his body and calling out to him. Here was a direct line of contact between the greatest and most noble people to have ruled this land and him-self. Feeling the weight upon his head, he took a pewter plate and cleaned it with a buffing motion on his sleeve. Then he stood up, erect and proud achieving his full height, closed his eyes and held the polished plate up in front of himself in readiness to admire his own countenance, now to be seen wearing the symbol of God's invested power here on earth. As he did so, Matthew mused this must be how a King felt the first time he wore the Crown of England at his own Coronation. Matthew opened his eyes and immediately dropped the plate onto the floor. The image he saw reflected in the pewter was of a misshapen grotesque mask of a man, a nose which was elongated and yet bulbous, a forehead high and narrow, eyes, both looking in different directions, a mouth which appeared twisted into a snarl of madness and the shape of his face looked like a monstrous parody of a human being. He did not see a regal figure; instead he saw a grotesque demon looking back at him. The crown itself still looked resplendent in its regal, majestic glory. Matthew took an involuntary step back from his unnatural and ugly image and tripped, falling headlong over the kilderkin he had placed on the floor. He lay there, shocked and stunned for a second or two, blood had drained from his face and he felt physically sick. This was the work of the Devil. Matthew immediately knew the curse of the Wrights had now become the curse of the Hopkins.

After a lying prone on the floor for a short while, the frightened and shocked man began to recover his shocked senses and with relief reasoned the distorted face he had seen reflected before him was only a trick of the candle light, an illusion perpetrated by the uneven surfaces of the pewter plate. Hopkins had used the pewter plate for years and he was sure the image he saw bore no resemblance in reality to his own features. Nevertheless, he could not shake the initial irrational impulse which had overwhelmed him; the curse of the Wrights had now been transferred to him.

Matthew was still on the floor, gathering his thoughts and then he realised the crown had rolled from his head and skittered across the floor. He regained his feet and walked shakily to where the crown lay, bent low and picked it up. Realising at that point how he had hit the kilderkin with some force and it had caused a nasty graze on his leg. He replaced the crown with the other jewels on the desk and sat on the chair, he looked down and rubbed his bleeding shin, glancing at the barrel he silently muttered an oath in its direction. As he rubbed his leg once again massaging a semblance of normality into it, he looked at the barrel, noting how it was still upright. He got up and went back to the table and decided to move it to a corner of the room where it would

MATTHEW AND THE KILDERKIN

be out of the way, unable to cause him any further injury. In his anger and frustration with himself for the thoughts he was having, he gave it a hefty kick and it skittled across the floor, coming to a halt against a wall. Once again it remained upright. Matthew looked at it again this time more inquisitively, he approached it and gave it another kick and it slid across the floor further but again it did not fall over. Matthew was now intrigued and went to the barrel and pushed it, he immediately noticed it was hard to push over, it was as if the bottom was weighted, but as he looked into the barrel, it was obviously empty. Matthew reached down and picked up the kilderkin and noticed that although it was empty, it was indeed bottom heavy. This time he upended the barrel onto the floor and attacked the bottom of it with some ferocity and once more found it quite easy to break loose the wooden base. This time he discovered a false bottom revealing a compartment about four inches deep. He returned to the desk and emptied the contents out alongside of the jewels. As he did so, he marvelled at the ingeniousness and craftsmanship of William Wright all those years ago. Matthew had not originally spotted anything untoward about the barrel after he had divested it of its contents and now the humble and unassuming kilderkin was revealing even more secrets which it had safely protected down through the centuries. All contained in a secretive and almost overlooked false bottom. After he had finished his further exploration he found he had three further objects on the desk in front of him. Each was wrapped in some kind of leather sheath which provided yet another layer of protection. Each one also had a waxen seal. The first felt like some sort of fabric through the protective leather, as his fingers were exploring he judged it was about a foot square and four inches thick and it had snuggled neatly into the bottom of the Kilderkin, almost filling the entire secret compartment. Matthew assumed this to be a Coronation robe of some sort. The other two sealed pouches were flat and seemed to be about the size of a document. Or small sheaf of letters, it was difficult to tell without opening them.

Matthew looked at the three additional wrapped and sealed parcels now lying side by side in front of him and slowly considered his options. After pouring himself a goblet of sack, he sat back in his chair and went into deep thought while absent-mindedly sipping at the sweet drink. After a lengthy internal debate with himself he decided the larger parcel must contain a vestment appertaining to a Coronation or similar ceremony and the two documents, if indeed that is what they were, would be purely of a historical Royal interest. As such, to Matthew there was no great pecuniary significance. As the seals were intact for the documents and the vestment, Matthew judged it to be a better gift to the Commonwealth if they could be seen to be unmolested and it would also prove he had not maltreated any of the finds he had in his possession. The Witchfinder decided this would be a far more judicious and prudent action to take, rather than just opening them now out of pure curiosity. Firstly, the garment would be of no use to him and even though he had studied Latin and could read and write it, he had no doubt any documents here would be a mixture of Latin, old English or old or legal French, so even if he tampered with the seals and opened the packets, he would probably not be able to read or interpret their meaning. No, better to leave well alone he reasoned. He also concluded they were probably something to do with the Coronation order of service or of some other historically religious meaning. No, it is definitely better to leave them intact. Hopkins sat down at the table before him and drew a detailed inventory of all that lay before him, then he

MATTHEW AND THE KILDERKIN

carefully copied the seal on the documents. Although he knew his artistic skills were lacking, he considered his attempt at drawing the seal was an adequate likeness. Maybe his friend John Thurloe could enlighten him when he advised Matthew on his course of action.

Matthew decided it would be far safer to hide the Jewels and documents for the very same reason William Wright had done all those years ago. People may come looking for them. The wrong people. Especially if word should leak from Westminster or through any of the many voices which could be heard prattling away in the corridors of Westminster Hall that the lost Crown Jewels of England had been found by Matthew Hopkins, as he felt sure was eventually bound to be the case. No, he needed to have them safe and sound. Matthew concluded every royalist sympathizer in the land would want to get them to King Charles or his brattling son and use them as a rallying point to raise the hopes of the people or worse still, attempt to raise another army. The jewels would not only become a potent symbol of a Royalty ready to return to what it saw as its rightful place, but more importantly they could be used as security for loans to raise foreign mercenaries to land on English soil and partake in prolonging these bloody Civil Wars. The very idea of hordes of warmongering Catholic mercenaries roaming amok across our treasured land was far more than he wished to contemplate. This was just one possibility. Of course some people would view the jewels with purely political intent but he might well find himself hunted down by soldiers of fortune, treasure hunters, common thieves and foreign governments. Even extreme puritans, who might well want this symbol of Royalty destroyed forever! Truly, the more he thought about the whole situation, the longer the list of reasons for hiding his find became. He hardly slept that first night, his mind in turmoil wondering if he was being pragmatic, practical or paranoid. Just for his own stillness of thought and peace of mind, he placed the kilderkin, with its precious hoard once again stored in situ, by the side of the bed and then he methodically loaded a flintlock pistol and placed it atop the barrel. Matthew slept easier. Even so he awoke during the night thinking he had heard a noise, lying still in bed he strained his ears as he stared intently into the darkness which surrounded him concentrating to see if the sound would repeat itself, but it did not, it was just the creaking of the old building. The pistol and barrel were as he had placed them. Matthew lay awake for a while with his proposed courses of action tumbling randomly around his brain. Eventually he reasoned what he had to do next. As a result, sleep came to him naturally as his mind drained itself of all other thoughts.

Chapter Nine

It was September 23rd and Matthew rode alone through the grey streets of Lynn. This time there was no escort or drummer and few people on the streets paid him any heed. Autumn was well established and it felt like the winter cold had arrived early in Lynn. The ride across the Fenland's had been uneventful and Matthew had appreciated the journey's solitude. It had enabled him to think more clearly about what lay ahead of him. Tomorrow were the sessions of the peace. He had returned to Lynn to give his evidence against those accused of witchcraft earlier in the year. Matthew would speak personally in the cases of Thomas Dempster, Cecily Taylor and Lydia Browne; his written evidence would be presented in the case of the remaining six witches.

The previous few days had been a flurry of activity for Matthew, he had decided he could not risk leaving his precious find at the Inn and certainly could not take it on the lanes and roadways of England with him, so he had hidden it. Matthew had re-wrapped the regalia, but this time in a new linen cloth. The three documents or whatever they should turn out to be, he bound in thin leather and sealed them in waxen pouches. Matthew knew they would not be hidden for too many weeks before John Thurloe introduced him to Oliver Cromwell and he revealed his find publicly to Parliament.

He then anticipated his star would shoot unconstrained up into the firmament. But, just in case something unforeseen happened, he thought it prudent to protect the cache as well as he knew how. Matthew had placed his precious hoard once more into a kilderkin, but this time he used one of the spare new ones from the cellar of the Inn. As he was preparing the new watertight cask he could not shake the thought from his mind that something might go wrong with his plan and the kilderkin could be lost forever. After all, it was not just the King's evil which stalked this land but the evil perpetrated by the Devil himself and Matthew knew he must be right at the top of that particular hate list! So once more the kilderkin had been consigned to a safe, dark place. Hopkins did not consider himself a vain man, just a Godlie, simple, plain soul who was doing the Lord's work here on earth. Although, he did feel his work was of far more importance than that of both his father James and of his brother John, who were both ministers. This also applied to his other brother, Thomas, who had been sent overseas to the New World where he was not only following, but spreading the word of the Lord. Matthew knew he was not just propagating the word of the Lord but was protecting the very essence of the word from the Demons and Devils who sought to make mischief with it at every opportunity. He was ridding the very earth of the scourge of Satan's minions, not just preaching against it. For this alone he would surely join the army of the saintly, sitting at the right hand of God. Matthew decided he would commit to paper the story which had led to this point in time and he assigned the completed letter to the kilderkin as well.

While writing his story, he was very conscious of his choice of words, some might say selective in what he included and what he left out, but Matthew reasoned to him-self, some-times the ends

MATTHEW AND THE KILDERKIN

justified the means. He knew he had no need to explain in great detail everything which had led up to his great discovery, for that was indeed what it had now become in his mind; his great discovery. He had been shown the way by God's hand, the hand that was always there to help him carry the banner for Christianity against the works of the dark one. He had broken the evil spell the Devil had placed on the Wright woman and had lifted the burden of the curse from her family. He had outwitted the very Devil himself. Her death would bring her salvation. Some might argue his methods were improper, he would say unconventional, but those same people have never had to face the wily ways of demons or outwit their manifestations in the human guise. He knew of their tricks and cursed ways, he alone could see through their ploys and he, Matthew Hopkins, was also clever enough to thwart them by whatever means he thought fit, unconventional or not.

By the hand of divine providence he would be able to restore the great treasures he had discovered to their rightful place in history. In fact Matthew was instrumental in making that very history. He would always be remembered for the restoration of the Crown and the Jewels to the people of England and alongside his work in witchfinding, he would always be revered. The honourable name of Hopkins would long be venerated, forever linked with words such as goodness, purity, honesty, fearlessness and piousness. Matthew Hopkins hoped this act, on behalf of the people of this great nation, would elevate him to the rank of General in both the army of Parliament and the army of the Lord. He could hear it now, people calling him General Matthew Hopkins, or Matthew Hopkins, Witchfinder General.

Matthew arrived in Lynn and received a warm welcome from the Landlord at the Inn and was given his old room. The Landlord was as ebullient as ever and was genuinely pleased to have Matthew back under his roof once more. Matthew had arranged for Miles Corbett to join him for dinner that evening and together they went through the evidence which would be heard at tomorrow's sessions. Alongside deciding the fate of the nine accused witches, the cases of two labourers, each accused as thieves, was to be heard, together with that of a thief who had been caught while on the run from London. It would be a busy day indeed. Miles was happy with the way in which Matthew had prepared his cases. Matthew chatted at length with Miles about the case of Lydia Brown. He told Corbett he felt his case against her was very weak and how his evidence might well mean her release. After all, as soon as she set foot into court room anyone would be able to plainly see that the Brown woman was obviously mad. In fact as mad as a March hare and people would see how she deserved to be helped and not punished. He would have no part in her unnecessary death. His conscience would be clear of this one deed at least. If her case went as anticipated, the authorities in Lynn would look foolish, so he proposed a compromise solution to Miles and he asked to have her committed to a place of safety where she could do no one any harm. Matthew would be happy to declare her non compos mentis and thus not fit to be tried. Miles Corbett thought this an admirable solution to a potential embarrassment.

The conversation turned to other matters and Miles told Matthew there was a tale of plague on the outskirts of Lynn. This alarmed Matthew as his good friend William Lilly the astrologer had predicted many apocalyptic prophesies for the last quarter of the year. Matthew was told many crops had already been trodden into mud and the usual sowing of wheat and rye in the area had practically come to a standstill. Surely, Miles reasoned, these catastrophes were all the legacy of the diabolists. Hopkins felt himself agreeing with the local man's assessment. After exchanging other news and views over a cordial meal, Matthew bade goodnight to the Recorder and retired.

The Monday sessions were packed and the atmosphere of a public holiday prevailed. He was shaken by the hand many times on his walk from the Inn to the sitting. It appeared many of the townsfolk were grateful for the work he and Stearne had done on behalf of the town and surrounding district. Matthew presented his cases against the nine accused, he had decided before his trip to the town how he would prosecute the case of Grace Wright. It was to be with gusto and full conviction. Knowing her death would be her only salvation and now that the curse had been lifted by him from her and her family, he could do no more than to save her soul. He quietly mused to himself how her death would also serve a second purpose.

Matthew liked Thomas Dempster and therein rested a problem. After all, Thomas had steered Matthew in the direction of the hidden kilderkin and he had also made it abundantly clear to Matthew how he bore him no malice if he was found guilty at today's sessions. Matthew knew the evidence against Thomas was not the strongest and reasoned that if he presented it without bias and with no recommendations or inflections, then Thomas may yet be saved from the hang-man's noose. That would be God's will. If his lover, the Godfrey woman was found innocent, then so be it. Thomas could lead the rest of his life happily in her arms. The other cases would stand or fall on their merits.

The hushed courtroom at the Trinity Guildhall was packed with onlookers as the cases were heard. When the cases against the suspected witches were heard, there was a palpable tension in the atmosphere. It was stated the indictment against Lydia Brown had been dropped as she was unfit to be tried. This news elicited general murmurs throughout the courtroom, some of an approving nature. Some were clearly unhappy the crowd would be deprived of watching a witch dangle at the end of length of hemp. Of this particular soul the Rope-man would be deprived. During the rest of the proceedings, there was the occasional groan, sharp intake of breath and looks of horror as the trials commenced, proceeded and testimony was given. Matthew noted the looks of awe on the faces of the people as he gave his evidence. He knew he was held more in fear than respect and yet people had a grim fascination with the proceedings as he did God's work on their behalf. He knew he was their champion. For some in the watching crowd, this would be the most exciting day of their lives, one which would be dissected and recounted countless times to friends, family, acquaintances and children for the rest of their lives. The accusers, watchers and keepers of the gaol all said their pieces where appropriate and with surprising rapidity. All too soon, the proceedings of the case of the nine witches had drawn to a conclusion. It was all over far quicker than most of the onlookers had anticipated. A short recess was announced, during which Matthew returned to the Inn and had a meal of cold meats and loblolly.

While he was eating, Joseph the carter had entered the Inn and respectfully stopped at his table inquiring as to his health. Matthew was happy to become re-acquainted with the man and asked him to join him; Joseph did this with much deference. It transpired Joseph's return journey from the Thorn Inn in Mistley had been uneventful, but since his return to Lynn, his luck had changed, he had begun to pick up work from the local garrison as well as two of the neighbouring estates. The carter put this down solely to his connection to the Witchfinder. He was very grateful to Matthew for trusting him with the job of transporting his possessions to Mistley and for the opportunities the job had opened up for him. He declared that if he could be of service to Matthew in the future, it would be his very great honour to oblige. Matthew replied how he might one day call upon Joseph's help again. This conversation heartened Matthew. He remembered fondly the long journey in the company of the friendly carter and how he had silently thanked him for his presence on the journey; after all it was his conversations with Joseph which kept his mind from speculating what the kilderkin might contain.

During his absence from the Trinity Guildhall, the sessions had reconvened and the cases of the three thieves had been heard. Matthew returned to his seat in time to hear the verdict of the returning jury in the cases of the nine witches of Lynn. The outcome was most unexpected. Of the nine, only two were found guilty. They were Dorothy Lee and Grace Wright. Hopkins smiled to himself at the declaration, but the other seven were all found not guilty. This verdict in the case of Thomas Dempster pleased him but the reprieved verdicts for Cecily Taylor, Katherine Banks, Lydia Browne, Emma Godfrey, Dorothy Griffin and Thomasine Parker mystified him. Why had there been such a change of heart in the people of Lynn. No matter, Matthew had completed his work here in the town to his own satisfaction. The verdict was not his to make or contradict. He had accused no one and had found no one guilty. His job was to interrogate, interview, collect and present evidence he found of witchery. This he had done and he had acquitted himself fairly, honestly and admirably. As the freed prisoners were released to go their separate ways, some were greeted by warm handshakes and hugs, others by dark mutterings and suspicious contempt. He watched Thomas Dempster leave the room out of the corner of his eye. Dempster left only giving the briefest of glances in his direction and none towards a hysterical Grace Wright.

Matthew was implacably staring straight ahead, his lips moving slightly in silent prayer for the souls of the two guilty women. He tried to block out the stream of abuse emanating from the two convicted witches as they were dragged away screaming, both hurling curses at the Witchfinder, their gaolers, accusers and watchers. Their cries were soon drowned by the general noise in the courtroom as they were hurriedly removed to the cells below their feet to await their execution in the morning. Matthew clearly heard Grace Wright calling him a thief and exclaiming he had stolen her treasure and he would writhe in hell alongside her. She screamed how she would summon up demons to torment his soul for eternity. She would not rest until she had proved her innocence from beyond the grave. Matthew continued to stare impassively forward. He knew that the few people who had heard the remarks would assume that they were the words of abuse the Witchfinder usually received from the foul mouths of the condemned. The very last time he heard Grace Wright's distant voice, it was plaintively calling out to Thomas Dempster, declaring her love for him. The hangings were set for the morrow when it was market day in King's Lynn and just like time, commerce and justice waited for no man. A Tuesday was as good a day to die as any other.

Matthew arose the next morning and settled himself in his usual seat at the Inn for his meal. He had been paid by the Mayor

MATTHEW AND THE KILDERKIN

of Lynn the previous day and had no further business in Lynn. He decided he would eat here in peace while it seemed the rest of the town and surrounding villages crammed themselves into the market place in anticipation of the hangings. The Landlord placed fresh warm bread in front of Matthew along with pork and soused sausages.

"We have all been up early today Master Hopkins, the kitchens have been busy preparing food and the cellar is full of beer!" he beamed. "It is usually pretty busy here on a market day but with two hangings as well, I'll be lucky if my food lasts until this evening," he said, while rubbing his hands briskly together in an almost childlike gesture.

Matthew needed a hearty start to the day to begin his long trek back to Mistley and the next stage of his personal adventure. The Landlord had been paid and he had made his excuses to Matthew after checking his guest did not require anything further and left to join the excited throng surrounding the market place. He knew it was probably too late to get a good view, but he had had the foresight to pay for a place on the wooden platform which had been erected against the side of St Margaret's Church. His view over the heads of the crowd would be ideal. His own space secure amongst the other tradesmen and people of influence in the town. He hurried out of the Inn, taking off his apron as he left, throwing it casually over the back of a chair by the door. Matthew was now alone. It seemed as if every soul in Lynn was in the market place waiting for the executions to take place. Matthew enjoyed the strangeness of being in an Inn in the centre of the full to bursting town, but being alone. The Inn was empty, as were the streets around it, save for the odd person who had arrived late, running towards the market place in the forlorn hope of getting a good place to stand. Although he was alone, he could hear the hubbub of the crowds in the distance and he knew this peace here in the Inn would be shattered in half an hour or so when it would become full of excited and thrilled townsfolk who wanted to discuss everything they had just witnessed, right down to the last shocking intimate detail, all debated over ale, bread, meats and cheese. It seemed strange to Matthew how the deaths of the two witches would create endless conversations in ale houses and Inns throughout the town, bringing friends together through the common event they had just witnessed. The Witchfinder knew that most Godlie people would be feeling relief now their community had rid itself of the pestilence of witchery. Matthew wondered how many people would be in the churches throughout Lynn praying for the souls of the executed women compared with those spilling out of the ale house doors.

"Master Hopkins Sir, I want to thank you."

Matthew looked up from his plate and saw a familiar figure standing before him, half silhouetted in the doorway. Returning to his food he said, "Why, Thomas Dempster, we meet again, this time in more conducive and fortuitous surroundings." Putting down his knife and wiping his mouth with the back of his hand, he looked the new arrival straight in the eye.

"Indeed we do Sir. Indeed we do," said Thomas impassively. "This time I greet you as a free man, albeit a free man with unfinished business."

"Oh," said Matthew curiously, raising an eyebrow and cocking his head to one side. "I was thinking our business had quite come to an end the moment you were released from custody." He put his hands on the table either side of his partially demolished plate of food, pausing before continuing with deliberately chosen words.

MATTHEW AND THE KILDERKIN

"You got what you wished for, the freedom of Mistress Godfrey and your good self. I'm afraid I could not save Grace Wright, from her crime. As you heard for yourself, the case against her was quite overwhelming and the jury could only return the one verdict, that of guilty. On the other hand, some might argue how your own case and that of Emma Godfrey were not prosecuted with all the vigour available to this particular witchfinder. As a result, you are now standing here in front of me instead of shitting yourself in your cold cell, waiting to meet your maker in ten minutes time." Matthew picked up his knife and carefully cut another piece of his soused sausage and lifted it to his mouth. "I owe you nothing Thomas, in fact you owe me your life and you owe me for the life of the woman you love. Not a bad outcome for you both was it? In the meantime, I had to endure your pitiful tale of curses and treasures." Matthew looked down and took a sup from his tankard and then raised his eyes once more to meet those of Thomas Dempster. "Alas Master Dempster, there was no curse of the Wrights, no great treasure, just a desperate woman with a sorry tale without foundation, one which had been passed down through her family for generations. As you can see, I am here before you having returned to Lynn to give evidence at your trial and I have my two pound fee in my pocket. If I had the treasure Mistress Wright spoke of in her desperation, I would not be gallivanting around the countryside in the cold and wet for a miserable two pound fee." Matthew let the logic of his words permeate into Thomas's mind. He raised his voice and continued, "Well Thomas? Would I? Would you, if our positions were reversed? I think not Master Dempster. I think not." With these words Matthew broke his gaze and looked down, picked up more sausage on his knife and started to eat it. He then looked towards Thomas and pushed his plate towards him and motioned for him to take one. "Forgive my manners Thomas, it has probably been a while since you have tasted sausage like this, please eat one."

Thomas was momentarily tempted with the offer of the food but then remembered why he was here, "You are a sneaky one Master Hopkins, I'll give you that. You use words well, I can only use my instinct and my instinct tells me you are lying."

"You have your freedom Thomas it goes along with your freedom to speak your mind. But do not test me." Matthew sat back in his chair and held his visitors gaze, "what else would you demand of me?"

"Fifty pounds sir, fifty pounds would be enough for Emma and my-self to leave this place forever and forget about witches, Matthew Hopkins, Grace Wright and Kings Lynn. It will buy us a fresh start in a new place. The treasure must be worth at least fifty pounds to you." said Thomas, hoping he had pitched his demand at the right level. He was convinced Hopkins was lying and had found Grace's curse. Thomas felt his one big problem was in assessing its value. Thomas had mentally placed a value of three hundred pounds on the treasure and guessed Matthew would be prepared to part with fifty pounds of it in return for his silence. "For that Sir, you have my word you will never hear from us again."

"What does your Emma think of her man extorting money from a man of God?" asked Matthew casually.

"She is not involved Sir, she knows nothing of this affair. At this very moment she is rejoicing in the bosom of her family."

All at once there was a thunderous cheer resounding from the market place, a cheer which lasted for fully half a minute then it just as suddenly became a hushed silence. Matthew knew Dorothy Lee had just been pushed from the ladder and was now dangling in the air. The cheer was for her fall. As she struggled on the gallows for her very life, kicking, convulsing and jerking as the rough hemp rope cut deeply into her exposed throat and neck. The crowd were being rapidly silenced by the enormity of watching someone die slowly and agonisingly in front of their eyes, her face starting to turn red and then blue. Some silently questioned to themselves, whether this was really an evil witch or just a poor wretch caught up in a situation beyond her control.

Matthew had pulled the pewter plate in front of him again as he returned eagerly to his food and without looking up said, "One down, now only one to go Thomas. If it was not for me, you may well have been the next to take the drop." Matthew raised his face and was smiling outwardly, a smile which Thomas mistook as that of a man satisfied with seeing his work come to completion. Matthew was in fact smiling at the fact Thomas had told him he was a lone agent in this affair. "Thomas, you have trusted me up until now, trusted me with your secret and your life and I have not let you down. Trust me once more and all will be well. You will be free to go to a much better place than Lynn. Meet me at the four mile stone on the Ely road at mid-afternoon and I will place a settlement upon you there, not because I feel indebted to you but rather for no other reason than I like you and would like to help you make a sound start with your new life. Now please go, it would be imprudent for us to be seen talking to each other at this time. I bid you good day Thomas Dempster."

Thomas held his hand forward; Matthew took it and shook it firmly. Thomas then turned on his heel and walked towards the door. A second cheer rent the quiet morning Norfolk air and Thomas stopped in his tracks. He knew he had just heard the death of Grace Wright. Thomas made the sign of the cross and felt his stomach churn then he hurriedly left the Inn. Matthew stuffed the remaining sausage into his mouth as he poured himself more ale from the pewter jug. Yes, thought Matthew, a Tuesday was as good a day to die as any other.

Indeed, both men thought this was a good day, but for very different reasons.

Chapter Ten

Matthew finished his business in King's Lynn within the hour and headed South on the Ely road. The Landlord had returned with his serving staff shortly after the final drop and almost immediately the Inn had filled as quickly as water filling a bowl from a bucket. The noise was unbearable, with men yelling to order their victuals and beer while excitedly shouting to each other about what they had just seen and heard, all in a confusion of arms reaching for ale and food amidst general laughter and merriment. Some people were now even singing and their friends started joining in. Matthew hated the carnival atmosphere which the hangings brought to a town, but he supposed it was a natural release of the tensions which had built up in a community which had the blight of witchery upon it. It also helped the local revenue and many were happy at this consequence. As he rode out of Lynn under the ominous grey Norfolk sky, his mind wandered from the noisy alehouses, equalled only in their business that day by the town's brothels, to his forthcoming meeting with Thomas. He did not pass another soul on the road. He knew it would be hours before the festive atmosphere in Lynn gave way to the reality of work and the lateness of the hour. Only then would groups of people start to make their way home towards the outlying villages before it got too dark. Matthew had plenty of time to meet Thomas, in secret, away from prying eyes.

As he approached the four mile stone, Matthew saw Thomas stood in the distance absent-mindedly blowing into his hands, warming them slightly against the chill afternoon air.

Thomas thought he was going soft against the cooling autumnal air and put it down to living in the shelter of the gaol for months on end. No fear, he would soon harden off to the weather once again. But with fifty pounds in his pocket, he and Emma could marry and would be able to afford a home of their own, maybe in Bristol or Plymouth. He had always fancied living in a sea port. He had heard there was plenty of work to be found in the docks of those great cities and it was far easier than the work he had been used to. But then again, with all that money, he need not work for years. Maybe he could create his own gang of labourers and sit back and take it easy while they did all the donkey work and he could become one of the dominant merchant classes. Surely this was to be his new position in life, his new destiny. The more Thomas thought about his future with Emma the more excited he became at the prospect and the more possibilities he could see stretching out before him. In these troubled times Thomas could see his life had at long last turned a corner and he would now begin to fulfil his potential. Having Matthew Hopkins enter his gaol cell a while ago was the best thing which had ever happened to him. Glancing up from the ground and shaken out of his day dream, he saw the solitary figure of Matthew Hopkins astride his horse plodding slowly towards him. He must also be feeling the coldness of the day he thought as he noticed how his hat was pulled down tightly and his cloak wrapped around him keeping out the chill Norfolk air. As Matthew's horse approached, Thomas walked towards the figure in greeting. When the two men were about ten paces apart, Matthew stopped his horse and dismounted, tying his reins to a small bush and walked the final few paces towards Thomas, with his right hand held before him in greeting. "Thomas, good afternoon," said a smiling Matthew Hopkins.

"Good day to you once again Master Hopkins," said Thomas holding forth his own hand to be shaken, full of anticipation and excitement about receiving his money and the bright future it ensured. What a handsome sum it was to be!

Matthew clasped his proffered hand and as he did so pulled Thomas towards him as he quickly raised his left hand from under his cloak. The loaded pistol was immediately and unhesitatingly discharged into the chest of Thomas Dempster. Thomas stood there grasping Matthew's hand in greeting, his mouth opening and closing noiselessly, trying to take air into his ruptured lungs, his eyes wide open in shock. He slumped to his knees and the pain, the worries, and the aspirations and life of Thomas Dempster ended as his grip of greeting relaxed and his hand fell limply to his side. All that remained was a bluish haze from the discharged weapon around the hole which punctured his clothing. This was mixed with the smell of black powder, fetid vegetation, and urine as Thomas pissed himself in death.

Matthew looked down at the crumpled heap on the muddy road and watched with detached interest as the dark patch of blood seeping from the hole in Dempster's chest widened, reddening his clothing until it eventually covered the front of his body. Matthew thought this was a much cleaner death than he could have imagined. For Thomas it was immediate and completely unexpected. It was at that moment Matthew wished for his own end to be like this. One moment Thomas was smiling and greeting him, full of life and dreams, in the next blink of an eyelid he was dead. Not even seeing the spark of the flint as it ignited the powder in the pan. Yes, Matthew decided he did like Thomas Dempster and was pleased he could do him this last service of ending his life in such a manner. Hopkins surmised that under different circumstances of geography and birth, he could easily have become friends with the still warm corpse now lying at his feet. Matthew drew the knife from his belt which he had earlier stolen from the Inn and leaned down over Thomas and firmly placed it into his hand, adjusting the fingers into a grip of aggression. All was now ready. Indeed, as he had reasoned to himself earlier, a Tuesday was as good a day of the week to die as any other.

Matthew did not have long to wait, within minutes three men rode quickly towards him from the direction of Lynn. They stopped their horses and dismounted.

"You were right then Master Hopkins," said a shocked looking Joseph as he peered down at the inert body lying crumpled on the ground.

"I'm afraid so Joseph," said Matthew impassively and gently shaking his head from side to side.

"Well I never thought I'd see the day when someone would try and take the life of such a great man as you sir," said the second man, who Matthew recognised as Joseph's brother, the man who had stood guard over his possessions during that long night in St Margaret's Church.

Joseph knelt down and turned the head of the prone figure lying on the floor towards the sky. Then he looked carefully into the face of the corpse, "It's him alright, it's Thomas Dempster." The other two men with him knelt and also identified Thomas's limp and pathetic looking body. Joseph then reached towards his chest

MATTHEW AND THE KILDERKIN 111

felt in vain for a heartbeat. Withdrawing his now bloodied hand from the dead man's chest he carefully wiped it clean of blood on Thomas's breeches. "He's dead alright."

"When you came to me this morning and told me you had been warned of rumours the witch Dempster was going to try and kill you I could scarce believe it sir, but you must have been in this position many a time before and I'm sure and know your business well enough to judge when to take such things seriously," said Joseph. "So I called upon my brother Josiah and my old friend Edmund and did as you requested and followed you. We all intended to follow you from Lynn to Ely to make sure you arrived all safe and sound."

"Joseph, Josiah and you Edmund, I thank from the bottom of my heart for following in my footsteps and affording me your protection." Matthew shook each man's hand in a gratefully firm grip.

The three men stood casually facing the Witchfinder in awe of his prowess at foretelling his own potential death. Their admiration of Matthew showed on their faces, they were pleased to have played some small part in his story.

"Dempster sprang out at me from behind the hedge at the mile stone marker and grabbed the reins of my horse. Then he held his knife to the poor animal's throat making me dismount. He told me he was about to kill me in vengeance for the death today of his first and true love, Grace Wright. The poor soul must have been beside him-self with utter despair and rage, watching his one true love die at the end of the rope-man's hemp. He left me with no other choice than to shoot him down with the pistol I had concealed beneath my cloak in case of such an occurrence." The three men were astounded at Matthew's display of understanding and compassion towards his assailant. "It was all so sudden; he lunged at me with the knife leaving me with no alternative but to discharge my shot into his chest. I fear if I had not done so, your arrival may have been too late and as we speak, one of you would be riding back to Lynn to inform the authorities of my own demise," Matthew said gravely.

"Don't you afear Master Hopkins; you are as safe as the Tower of London now, Thomas Dempster is no more of a threat to you than a passing cloud now he's dead. I know he was once a walking out with Grace Wright and he had loved her so very much. Some say she bewitched him, I have no idea: mayhap he had become bewitched by her. Maybe her vengeful spirit was trying to kill you from beyond the grave and was using his hand," with that the other two men slowly looked at each other and shivered, realising the power the Devil might still have over his servants, even in death.

"Well gentlemen," said Matthew Hopkins drawing himself erect. I suppose we will have to return to Lynn to explain ourselves. I presume that will take time and will prove to be an inconvenience to the four of us. I have other appointments to keep of an urgent nature; I am expected at Ely for the trial at the assize of the three witches, Disborough, Garrison and Green, so we had better start back for Lynn now, although I suspect everyone will be dealing with drunkards and rebel rousers at the moment, damn!" Matthew cursed. "I may have to wait around for a couple of days to enable me to speak at length to the Chief Justice. These delays will be very inconvenient for the good souls of Ely and beneficial for the Devil, allowing his servants to do their worst.

The three men looked at each other, "Well Master Hopkins," said Joseph tentatively, "we could always take care of things here and let you get on your way and help the good folk of Ely, if you want us to that is sir"

"After all," said Josiah, taking up his brothers theme, "begging your pardon sir but we all know what happened here sir, as plain as the day is long. No case to answer. We could fetch up Dempster's body and take it back to Lynn, for you sir. The only thing is Joseph and I have some outstanding family business we should like to attend to ourselves, with a cousin, so we would have to take Dempster with us on a small detour so as to speak."

"Family business?" inquired Matthew.

"Yes sir, out on the fens, we were going to see to it on the way home from Ely but, well we are almost there now, so while we are out here, we may as well kill two birds with one stone so as to speak."

"My brother is right sir," smiled Joseph. "We will see our cousin and then deliver a report to the Magistrate when we get back to Lynn. No need to inconvenience you any further Master Hopkins."

"It will soon be getting darker Joseph, the nights draw in quickly at this time of the year, are you sure you will be alright in the fens in the dark?"

"Why bless my soul Master Hopkins, what a kind hearted soul you are, it is a journey we have made many a time. We usually take him supplies on a packhorse. We have only ever lost the goods once in the dark, plop into the mud and water they went and we were never able to find them again," smiled Joseph.

"I'm sure that won't happen again to us sir. We would hate to lose Thomas in such a way," smiled Josiah.

"That's right isn't it Edmund," said Joseph as he discreetly winked at Edmund.

"You're right Joseph it would be very unfortunate, very unfortunate indeed. I'd never forgive myself if Thomas was to go amissing in the dark, consigned to the mud and the bogs and deprived of a proper Christian burial."

The three men smiled at the Witchfinder and Joseph said, "Then all be settled Master Hopkins. You carry on about your business and leave the rest to us; we will make sure all is right here in Lynn."

Matthew knew what the three men were going to do and decided to say nothing; after all it would be the answer to everyone's problem, especially his. Matthew reached into his purse and retrieved three coins, one for each man. "Gentlemen, I cannot thank you enough for being my protectors. I realise you put your lives at risk in agreeing to help me with my problem this afternoon and this but is a small token of my appreciation," he said, as he handed each man a silver coin. "I trust you find your cousin well and you have no mishaps or misadventures in the dark while out on the fens. Joseph, you and your companions are good men and your deeds here today will not be forgotten, you will always be welcome to join me in food and ale at the Thorn Inn in Mistley," said Matthew, as he once again held forth his hand to each man in turn and he received three vigorous, appreciative and enthusiastic hands in return.

Matthew mounted his horse and with cries of "Good luck and God's speed," ringing in his ears set off on the road to Ely. He looked back after a quarter of a mile and saw no sign of anyone. It was as if this grey, silent world of the fens had swallowed them up. Matthew gave a small involuntary shiver, pulled his hat down tighter onto his head and wrapped his cloak closer. Then without another look back towards Lynn, he spurred his horse onwards. This had been a good day. I like Tuesdays he thought to himself.

Chapter Eleven

The autumn proved to be as catastrophic as William Lilly, the famed astrologer, had predicted. Not only were there fears about plague and crop failures throughout the land but the tide appeared to be turning against Matthew and his works. It seemed it was now getting harder to achieve fewer convictions. There were also dark rumblings from certain quarters about the legality and worth of his work. His main antagonist was John Gaule, the vicar of Great Staughton. Earlier this year he and Stearne had been questioned in Norfolk about their methods and their fees. The very gall of it! Yes, the climate was definitely changing.

Matthew was confident the year of 1647 would bring him prosperity and a new direction in his life. A New Year heralded a new beginning. It seemed impossible that Matthew and John Stearne had only embarked upon their crusade such a short time ago. His records showed him around three hundred witches had been found guilty and were executed during this time. The first was in March 1644, such a short time ago. He remembered being told by one Recorder how he and Stearne had sent more witches to their deaths than all other witch-hunters in the previous one hundred and sixty years. Matthew was very proud of this fact. He remembered how, at the age of just twenty four, when his crusade started, he knew his destiny was yet to be fulfilled. Now at almost twenty seven, he knew the time had come to move on and embark upon the next phase in what he knew was already an extraordinary life. It was now time to retire. Maybe he would write a book or two.

Matthew had much correspondence with John Thurloe and had asked many times for his old friend to arrange a meeting with Oliver Cromwell, a meeting which Matthew promised would be to his great advantage. He knew Cromwell had been ill during February and had dropped out of the public eye but each reply was much the same, telling him how Oliver Cromwell was tied up in matters pertaining to the New Model Army or with State or Parliamentary duties and was unavailable to meet with him at this time. Matthew was beginning to feel desperate when in June he received a letter of response from John Thurloe inviting him to London in July for a meeting. This was the chance Matthew had been waiting for. He had thought and brooded for months about what he should say and how he should broach the subject of the Crown Jewels with his old friend. Matthew felt at long last, his time had come.

Although it was the summer, Matthew was feeling unwell and the road to London was long and lonely. He was extremely nervous about his forthcoming meeting with his old friend, John Thurloe. Matthew had a pony with him carrying the supplies and equipment he needed for the journey. He decided to visit the Parish of his father, James Hopkins. It was only a short detour from his route. From this stop he would not only gain spiritual strength, but he knew his father could help him still, even in death. He made the short trip to his father's old parish at Great Wenham, about eight miles distant from Mistley. This had been home to Matthew as a young man and he had been born here. He cast his eye with remembered fondness around the few scattered house of the village before going to the church of St John. He looked at the beautiful half-timbered house by the church which he remembered affectionately from his youth. It was as if he was only here yesterday, memories of friends and family came tumbling into his consciousness. Childhood play and first loves and hot long summers alternating with cold sharp winters. He dismounted, took the burden from the pony, after all it held great wealth. He then entered the church.

After establishing he was quite alone, he leafed through the Hopkin's family bible which his father had bequeathed to the parish. He was proud to see it on display and still being used, sitting solidly on the lectern, from where he had given many readings for his father over the years. He huddled over the good book, busy at his work. Matthew prayed in the church for a while, remembering the village and its people, soaking in the atmosphere of the place his father had devoted his life to. He always loved the smell and the lightness of the space. This was a place where the tranquillity of his childhood reigned supreme. He could never have imagined the course his life would take after having left this place. He found his father's grave in the churchyard and stood beside it; head bowed and then he made a silent prayer to James Hopkins, his departed father. Looking at the inscription, showing James died in 1634, Matthew could scarce credit his father had already been gone from him for a dozen or so years. He placed his pack on the floor as he bent his head in prayer. Setting about his self-appointed task, his mind wandered and he silently wondered what his father must have thought of his other son John, who had been appointed as Minister in South Fambridge in Essex just last September, in fact around the time when Matthew was meeting with the accused witches at

King's Lynn, a meeting which this very day was to take him on the road to London. Matthew knew his brother John to be feckless and irresponsible. He had already heard tale from Essex how his brother was neglecting his work in the Parish. If he did not buck up his ideas, he would have both his brother and God to answer to!

It had been a goodly while since Matthew had thought of his family, but standing here beside his father's grave it seemed the natural thing to do. It was time to go. Great Wenham may yet be my salvation he mused to himself as he untethered his horse and pony and mounted his mare and started his journey towards the greatest city in the land. He felt he could do no more at this stage but to meet with John Thurloe and through him put his story to Oliver Cromwell himself. All had been prepared.

A few days later Matthew arrived in the early evening at the house of his friend, John Thurloe. As he approached the city he was amazed at how much building work was going on, the city was certainly growing and along with it, its power, wealth and influence. Matthew instinctively felt safe here, as London had never wavered in its support for the Parliamentarian cause.

"Matthew, it is a pleasure to have you once again in my home," said Thurloe striding directly towards Matthew hand outstretched to grasp that of his old friend. Matthew was welcomed into the candle lit, oak lined room, "and how was your journey?" Thurloe observed his friend in the candle light and noted his ashen pallor. "My friend you look awful, are you unwell?" he asked in a concerned manner.

Matthew laughed at his remark and was about to brush it to one side but the laugh brought about a coughing fit. When it subsided he said, "The journey was long but uneventful, as for my health I have a cold and have been feeling unwell for a week or so."

MATTHEW AND THE KILDERKIN

Matthew smiled and continued in a more positive vein, "The ride through our wonderful countryside has once again made me realise how lucky we are to be alive, even during these troubled times."

"Well, to be sure, these are interesting times indeed," smiled John Thurloe. "Nathaniel!" Thurloe bellowed, the noise of which brought a sprightly young man into the room. "Ah Nathaniel, please arrange to stable and feed Matthew's horse and pony, then bread, sac, apples and a cheese board for my guest and I," he told the young man. "Nathaniel has been with me for a couple of years now Matthew; I'm not sure what I'd do without him. He assists me with my business and runs my house here in London. Nathaniel, after you have finished those tasks please convey Matthew's bags up to his room."

Three hours of good sac, cheeses from the shires of the Kingdom and freshly baked bread with its uniquely comforting aroma accompanied their conversation and reminiscences as the two men sat before the fire and warmed their feet. They discussed current affairs, politics, and Matthew's work and talked of old friends and of course, God.

"Nathaniel has prepared a bed for you Matthew and I have arranged an audience with Master Cromwell in the morning. You have come at a fortuitous time. Oliver has just received good news about the King, he is no longer being held by the New Model Army but by Thomas Fairfax. He is in a good mood. You indicated secrecy, so Oliver will attend upon us here in my home mid-morning."

"Thank you John," said Matthew warmly.

"Would you like to tell me what you wish to discuss with him? Your letters have been vague on that subject, but I detected a sense of importance and urgency."

"My dear friend, I dare not talk to anyone of my reason for my visit to London before I have spoken with Master Cromwell. You will understand why on the morrow. I know you gather intelligence for the Army of Parliament and Master Cromwell, tomorrow you will have much to ponder, trust me my friend he will thank you for introducing us."

The two men eventually retired for the night, their friendship stronger than ever after their convivial evening spent sharing each other's thoughts and companionship. Both men liked each other.

Chapter Twelve

John and Matthew arose early and prayed together before eating a hearty breakfast of pickled fish. Thurloe had Nathaniel prepare the new and expensive delicacy of coffee which was becoming fashionable amongst the well connected within the merchant classes of the City. Matthew had heard of the beverage but this was the first time he had tried it. Although the smell was not unpleasant, he did not enjoy the bitter drink but out of courtesy told his friend the contrary. Thurloe called for Nathaniel and excused himself as he had work to complete. The two men left and attended to their day's business in the neighbouring study, leaving Matthew alone in the room. Matthew found it hard to relax but did his best. He took a book from the shelf and sat by the window to read. He enjoyed the pages he read, he was stimulated by bouts of enlightenment interspersed with glancing upwards, fascinated by the sight of the life blood of the City flow effortlessly past his vantage point in the street beyond the window. He sensed he could not be able to spend his life in such a ceaselessly busy place as London. Business or friends which brought him to the capital would be fine, but to live here deserved an emphatic no. He knew the open skies and tracts of the eastern counties were his true home.

He mused that it was right and proper a man should know his correct place in God's grand scheme. God had chosen well for him.

He seemed to sense before he heard the sound of horse approaching and looked out of the window to see five horsemen approaching. Four of them he observed as being russet coloured troopers of the New Model Army, probably trusted veterans he thought as they stopped in an orderly fashion outside the house. The fifth man was dressed in the stark black and white raiment of a puritan, his hat being pulled low and his face discretely cast down. All the men dismounted save for one trooper. He took the reins of the other horses and his head started to swivel, watching carefully the people in the street as they bustled about their business. The remaining four men approached the house. Matthew heard the ensuing knock and heard the door open. Leaning forward in his seat he watched through the window as the men entered into the house. Their voices became clearer, the door to the room opened and a trooper, hand on pistol entered the room and looked around suspiciously, he then walked towards Matthew and said, "Excuse me Sir, would you please stand up," Matthew did as asked and the trooper proceeded to professionally, yet discreetly search his body and then, just as swiftly he retreated. Matthew heard the trooper announce the room was clear and Nathaniel, John and Oliver Cromwell entered. The door closed silently behind them.

"Matthew, I am pleased to meet you," said Cromwell warmly as he walked towards Hopkins. "John here has told me so much about his old friend from his youth and of course we are very impressed with the good works you have been performing for us in the eastern counties."

MATTHEW AND THE KILDERKIN

Matthew blushed slightly. Thurloe mentally noted this was the only colour he had seen in his old friends cheeks since his arrival "I am only discharging my duty to God Master Cromwell."

"I hear tell your duty is discharged and prosecuted with vim and vigour," he said as he removed his cloak, Nathaniel approached and silently took it from his outstretched hand.

"That will be all Nathaniel," said Thurloe curtly. Matthew noted that in the presence of Cromwell, John's demeanour had changed, being more deferential and business-like. The three men were now alone and they sat at the table in the middle of the room.

"I'm sorry you were searched Matthew, in these troubled time I find it a necessity, after all we are at war with half the country and you can never tell where your enemy might lie," he said as he carefully eyed the infamous witch pricker. "I am off to a meeting with my officers in the Trained Bands," he said, "So I'm afraid we must get straight to the point. John tells me you have long sought this private meeting with me. I will tell you now, I rarely conduct business like this, I prefer things to be open and above the board, all to be transparent and conducted in the light of the day and under the full gaze of God, but I trust John's judgement, so I have come. Now, out with it, what do you require of me?" Both men turned their full gaze onto Matthew, who felt him-self redden at the collar once more.

"Sir, I have something of wonderful import to tell you. A series of objects have recently fallen into my possession, great treasures from the past."

John Thurloe leaned in towards Matthew and asked cautiously, but with barely disguised curiosity coming through in his voice. "What sort of treasure Matthew?"

"A treasure which will secure forever the position of Master Cromwell as the head of State," he replied lowering his voice. Leaning slightly towards Cromwell he continued, "I have heard rumours which tell of the Parliament intending to offer you the crown of England when this accursed Civil War and the fate of the King has been resolved."

Oliver looked conspiratorially at John and then turned his head back in the direction of Matthew, "And pray, tell me where you have been hearing such unfounded rumours Matthew?" he asked.

"They are discussed over dinner in many fine houses they are also whispered in the court rooms and markets of Anglia and are openly talked of in the alehouses."

"Ah, I forgot the gossip of old wives and men in their cups. John told me you were a tapster!" he teased.

Matthew decided to let the remark pass without comment. "If there is any substance or credence at all in these rumours, then the treasure I hold will confer the position as being rightfully yours. If not, then there are many objects which you can dispose of as you see fit, for they are very valuable, indeed some might even say they are worth a King's ransom."

Matthew stood and walked across the room to a long leather bag he had brought earlier down from his bed chamber. He placed it on the table, reached into it and withdrew his hand. It contained a long object wrapped in plain white linen. Making no comment, Matthew began to un-wrap the article. "Sir, I am no historian, nor do I presume to be an expert on antiquities, but I think this is the Sceptre used by King Edward the Confessor at his Coronation and it is part of the Royal Crown Jewels lost by King John in 1215, four hundred and thirty odd years ago." As he said these words he

MATTHEW AND THE KILDERKIN 127

delicately unfolded the last vestige of the linen shroud revealing for only the second time in over four hundred years the golden Sceptre topped with a dove.

Silence reigned.

All three men looked at the bejewelled object in awe. It glistened and shone with stones of many colours reflecting dazzling reds, blues, yellows and greens onto the ceiling and into the room as the sun light from the window hit it. The last time Matthew revealed the Sceptre it had been by candle light, but this was so very different. The sapphires, diamonds, rubies and emeralds came alive, dancing in all their splendour and subtlety before their very eyes. None of the men present had seen anything as beautiful as this vivacious ornamentation. The Sceptre was lying in its wrapping of white linen before them on the table in this otherwise sparse, plain chamber, a room now alive with reflected pin pricks of vibrancy, bouncing off the walls and ceiling.

"Where did you get this Matthew?" asked John Thurloe, not taking his eyes from the Sceptre lest it should evaporate.

Matthew had known this question would come and responded with a well-rehearsed half-truth he hoped would satisfy the two men. Matthew had decided as part of his plan to tell as much of the truth as he dared, in the hope this would make his account more convincing and sound more honest. You can't be tripped up in a truth. He took a deep breath and began his narrative with barely supressed apprehension, telling them how it had been offered to him as a bribe by a suspected witch in return for her freedom. Both John and Oliver immediately recognised this scenario as they had both been in similar positions and knew of the promises of gold, land or riches which desperate people would make in return for their freedom. Matthew Hopkins went on in a clear and steady voice to tell them how the woman told him she had never seen the treasure herself but its secret had been passed down through many generations of her family. He related how she claimed all she knew was that a family heirloom was supposed to exist buried beneath a tree in a village on the fens. Matthew told the men how he had been told many such tales over the years and none had ever once swayed him from his duty. He noticed both men were imperceptibly nodding their heads in agreement at this part of his tale. Matthew continued, stating the witch was fairly tried and duly hanged for her abominations. Months later while travelling, he had found himself near the village mentioned by the witch and had found the tree she had so earnestly described and simply dug into the earth and this is part of what he found.

Both men seemed totally satisfied with the story he had spun from the truth.

"Matthew," said Cromwell quietly, his eyes looking up from the Sceptre and into the face of the storyteller, "Did you say part of what you found?"

"Yes Master Cromwell, there were other fine objects, some swaddled and sealed and some like this Sceptre lightly wrapped. There were four gold rings, two of which have fine stones. An amulet worked intricately in gold, two crucifixes, this golden Sceptre and a matching orb in silver, which has become much tarnished over the years. An Ampulla which I presume must have been used to anoint the Confessor at his Coronation. There were also three sealed and heavily waxed leather packages. I judge one to contain a garment, probably a robe used at the ceremony and two which appeared to hold letters. These may be the order of service or some other important State or Church document from the time. I am sure John and his fine team of intelligence gatherers will have

MATTHEW AND THE KILDERKIN

no difficulty in researching and confirming the hoard which I now have in my possession as being that of the Royal Crown Jewels lost by King John in the Wash all those years ago." Matthew reached into the folds of his doublet and produced a sheet of paper, the one he had drawn up when he first examined the kilderkin. "Here is a full list of what I found and here is an accurate copy of the waxen seal. I am sure you will find it belongs to King John or King Richard."

The two men were stunned into silence. Matthew guessed correctly that many thoughts must be tumbling through their heads. Which items they might decide to sell in order to finance their aims? Which could be used to legitimise Cromwell's position? He could just imagine how their heads were swimming with possibilities.

Oliver looked up again from the Sceptre into Matthews eyes and asked quite calmly, "Where is the rest of the treasure Matthew?"

"I have it well hidden, where it will not be found for another four hundred years," he smiled. "I hid it realising if anyone should become aware of its existence every rogue, vagabond, mercenary, foreign government and Royalist sympathiser in Europe would be beating a path to my door. I had to ensure it was safe for both you and the Parliamentarian cause." Matthew covered his face with a kerchief and coughed involuntarily for a few seconds. "I'm sorry gentlemen, I am not in the fullness of health at the moment, too many years and miles on horseback in the wet and cold I'm afraid." The other two men smiled knowingly and nodded in assent, both having suffered from the same predicament over the years!

"You have done well Matthew," said John Thurloe, looking into the face of his friend.

"Very well indeed," repeated Oliver Cromwell.

"There is one more object which I have failed to mention."

Both men looked surprised and turned their gaze upon the Witchfinder. "What might that be?" inquired Thurloe, breaking the heady atmosphere.

"The lost crown of Edward the Confessor," said Matthew triumphantly.

Matthew settled back comfortably in his chair and watched the reaction of the other two men. He could read nothing on their faces. Both were men of State and knew how to hold an unrevealing face. Were they gloating? Plotting? Dreaming? He surmised he would never find out.

"There is no one on this earth besides you who knows of the whereabouts of the remaining pieces?" asked Thurloe incredulously.

"No one John, I and only I, know of its current resting place."

"Tell me Master Hopkins, you would want what in return for these treasures?" said Oliver Cromwell sitting back in his chair at last, eyeing up the man before him. His attention was now focussed on the man and not the trinkets.

"Well Sir," Matthew had thought of his answer to this question many times on his ride to London and knew just what to say. "Firstly, I want you to understand I believe totally in the aims of the Parliamentarian cause. It will be an honour to return these valuables to your hands for safe keeping and I will watch with eagerness how you use or dispose of them as you deem most likely to benefit our cause. I know with God's guidance you will assuredly do the right thing."

"Tell me Matthew, why did you not take this tale to the Kings supporters on the Continent or get word to him at Holdenby

House? This information would be warmly received in both those quarters I am sure."

"Sir, I fear I have not made myself properly understood, I am utterly loyal to the Army of Parliament and the cause for which it fights. I abhor the King and his evil advisors and what they all represent." Matthew stood erect and raised his voice and his head and loudly proclaimed, "No Bishops, no Kings, just King Jesus!"

Oliver allowed a small smile to escape onto his face. "So pray tell Matthew, what exactly do you want in exchange for them?" asked Cromwell, staring right into Matthew's soul through his eyes. For an instant Matthew was shocked to find him-self very afraid. The moment passed as quickly as it had come. "Do you petition me for estates, power or wealth?"

"Master Cromwell I truly desire nothing. A small pension and somewhere fine to live in the City to enable me to perform any future services to Parliament as they should deem fit to entrust me with, would be more than ample reward for my small service to you and to the country." Matthew judged if he asked for little he would be rewarded with more. Matthew was not naturally a gambling man but had lived and relied upon his instincts and he felt secure in the knowledge he was dealing with two men who were both intrinsically honest and honourable.

Cromwell studied the pallid face of the Witchfinder who now sat patiently and calmly before him. After a short while he leaned forward in his seat, "Parliament and the cause could do with more men like you Matthew, men who have proven themselves to have been of a truly worthwhile and practical service to their nation." A long pause ensued as he sat back in his chair and pondered the situation, his hand gently rubbing his cheek. As if reaching a sudden conclusion he leaned forward earnestly in his seat and declared, "I see your future lying in politics. Tell me Matthew, have you ever considered your life as a Member of Parliament?" Oliver said slowly, ruminating on the possibility.

"Sir I will serve my country as you feel befits my industry and talent. I fear I have neither the wealth nor status to become a member of the House."

"Leave that to us to sort out, eh John! We all need friends in great places of power," smiled Oliver Cromwell looking to Thurloe. Both men smiled conspiratorially.

John Thurloe stood, laughed and slapped his friend on the back. "You have done very well this day Matthew."

"I read your recent pamphlet entitled, "The Discovery of Witches," and was enlightened by its content. I note the woodcut thereupon refers to you as Matthew Hopkins, Witchfinder General, not a title you have the right to bear I fear," said Cromwell noting what little colour there was in Matthews sallow face draining rapidly.

"Master Cromwell, please let me explain. For the pamphlet, I undertook to commission a fine wood block, illustrating both my work and a likeness of myself. When the block arrived it was titled as you saw. We had little choice but to impress the pamphlet and so the mistake was immortalised in print. I know I had no right to use such a title, an honest mistake Sir and one not intended to misrepresent or inflate my position."

"No doubt, no doubt, but I understand that since then all and sundry now call you the Witchfinder General, well Matthew, let us make the title official as from now. I think for your endeavours in removing the scourge of witchery from the east of our land, your services deserve true recognition." Cromwell smiled and looked pleased with himself, he continued, "Of course you would have to be gracious enough to accept the remuneration which would go with the rank of General. I am sure we can arrange this matter when we have taken delivery of the rest of the treasure. Then we can also see about expediting your position as an elected member of the Parliament."

Matthew's heart leaped. He had been referred to by folk as Witchfinder General for a while due to the mistake with the printers, but now his title was to become official and with a General's pay! What a day. This news was far better than he had expected to hear. Cromwell and Thurloe had just promised to bestow favours on him he could only have imagined. He knew that in becoming a sitting member of the Parliament he would need assistance both financially and socially and here was freely being given promise of both. He had succeeded. God had rewarded him here on earth for doing his will. His future prosperity and the name of his family would live forever. He would be known and remembered as Matthew Hopkins, who had single handedly restored King John's lost treasure from the Wash. Matthew Hopkins, Witchfinder General. Matthew Hopkins, Member of Parliament. He could only guess at how proud his father James would be if he were alive to share this glorious moment.

Chapter Thirteen

Cromwell and Thurloe were alone. They had asked Matthew to step out of the room telling him they had affairs of state to discuss before Oliver left for his meeting.

The room had assumed and icy chill. "Tell me John, your friend Matthew. What do you think?" pondered a serious looking Oliver Cromwell.

"He must be killed and killed quickly," said a solemn looking John Thurloe.

"Of course he must. Death is the only option," said Oliver grimly. "He is close to you; do you feel comfortable in making the arrangements?"

"I have caused those who have been far closer to me to die" he replied coldly. "He is a friend and so I will give him the courtesy of performing the undertaking personally, I owe him as much."

Chapter Fourteen

August 1647

The long hot days of August had arrived and although Matthew's illness had not yet left him, he had other thoughts to occupy the long days and nights in Manningtree. Matthew's furtive expectations had barely abated since his recent visit to London and his secret encounter with Oliver Cromwell and his good friend John Thurloe. His mind had been alive with making plans and mentally exploring the new possibilities for his future. His old friend John Stearne had visited him earlier in the year for a couple of days and the two men reminisced and laughed about some of their exploits together. John Stearne had often been referred to as the Witch-hunter or the Witch-pricker, two titles he had relished, but he was now a little jealous of the fact Matthew was being hailed as Witchfinder General. John thought this a more appropriate title than his own epithets, more in standing with their vocations. He felt jealous; Matthew's position had become legitimised, whereas his own titles were just crude nick-names. Like Matthew, John had also retired and now lived peacefully enough with his family in the village of Lawshall about thirty miles north of Mistley, near Bury St Edmunds. He proudly told Matthew that his name was widely celebrated throughout the district and he was now more famous than Ambrose Rookwood, who had been a native of the same village. Rookwood was renowned for breeding horses and was invited to join the infamous Gunpowder Plot. It was thought his horses might well be a useful asset to the conspirators to help with their escape. Rookwood was arrested and later executed in 1606 for his part in the plot. Matthew had first met John Stearne in Manningtree, a prosperous market town surrounded by a mixture of forbidding marshes, woods and farmland, a few years earlier in 1644 when Stearne, who was his senior by ten years and a seasoned witchfinder to boot, appointed him as his assistant. A fact which irritated Matthew every-time Stearne brought it up. The retired John Stearne worked his piece of land which he owned, his days of witchfinding now behind him. He confided to Matthew how he was considering writing a book which he intended to call, "A Confirmation and Discovery of Witchcraft." After Stearne's departure, Matthew judged the idea of writing about his experiences was a great idea and unknown to Stearne he immediately started work upon his own volume. His subsequent book, "The Discovery of Witches" had sold well and he had also used it as a vehicle to answer his critics. He had stolen yet another march on John Stearne. His own book was published and being read while Stearne was still busy thinking about the idea while tilling his land. Stearne always fell within his shadow and would continue to do so he thought to himself contentedly.

Vanity and pride were two sins which Matthew tried hard to suppress but sometimes he just could not help himself. He repeatedly reprimanded himself about these two weaknesses but even so he remained in a state of heady excitement about his future. It was around the beginning of August he received the long anticipated letter from John Thurloe. It was short and succinct,

MATTHEW AND THE KILDERKIN

informing Matthew he would arrive within the week to finalise all, to everyone's mutual satisfaction.

This was a time of much illness throughout the country and Plague had broken out in areas of London. Even the colleges in Cambridge had been closed to prevent the spread. Matthew was still ailing and had taken to his bed at home in Manningtree. Everyone fussed over him, although he tried to brush them aside as you would an angry wasp, deep down he was pleased they all showed so much care and affection for him. He had never felt this poorly. Just when his dreams were coming to fruition his own body was letting him down. Matthew prayed for his return to health with a fervour he had never known, after all he was only twenty seven and was years away from his prime. He should be in rude health.

His friend arrived at his home in Manningtree on August 11th and upon being shown up to Matthew's bedroom John Thurloe was shocked at the state in which he found him. When he entered the bedroom he could immediately make out the faint aroma of onions which pervaded the room. John knew this smell usually accompanied pleural tuberculosis. He had smelled it many times before. Although John Thurloe had come to kill his old friend Matthew Hopkins, he guessed the poison he had brought with him may not be needed.

Matthew was in a good mood and genuinely rallied at the presence of his companion. The two men spent the next few hours deep in conversation, Matthew asking many questions about what his duties as a Member of Parliament might entail and where he might stand as a member, he was eager to learn all the gossip and intrigue of the City. Soon this would be his stock in trade. Inevitably the conversation turned to the treasure.

"You do not seem fit enough to me to go out with a spade digging up a Kings lost Crown," smiled John. "Your time would be better spent here in bed!"

"No sir, I admit I am not as fit as I should be, but all will be well soon," smiled Matthew. Speaking these few words caused Matthew to cough and hold a rag to his mouth. John helped the ailing man to lean forward while he adjusted the bolster to make his companion more comfortable. As he did so he took the opportunity to straightened the blankets, John noted spots of blood on the rag Matthew was holding and felt genuinely sorry for his old friend. "But I'll be fine in the morning! I always rally in the mornings after a good night's sleep," he laughed. Matthew was convinced this current bout of illness would only last a few days, but John was thinking otherwise. Matthew held up his hand and John clasped it. He nodded in the direction of the bedside table where a letter lay tucked beneath the candle holder. "In case I should not be able to guide you to the treasure I have committed the place to paper."

"That is unnecessary Matthew, we will fetch it together in a few days when you are feeling better," said Thurloe. I can wait for your health to improve. After a pause John continued, his eyes looking at the letter. "Is this the only copy of its hiding place? You have told no one else?" asked John anxiously.

"My friend, you, Oliver and I are the only ones who even know of its existence. I am the only one who knows where it is hidden; it is safe under the watchful eye of my father who is now in heaven. I suppose it could be found in the word of God, where all things may be discovered." Matthew smiled at this and continued. "Be assured, this letter will reveal the location to you and you alone."

John gently slid the sealed letter from beneath the candle holder. "My dear old friend, we will wait a couple of days until you are over this illness and we will collect it together." As he said these words, John Thurloe took the letter and studied it. He noticed the seal was unbroken. Then he held it gently in the steady flame of the candle. After a second or two the letter caught alight and both men looked in silence as he slowly and deliberately turned the letter, letting the flames climb and eat into the paper to devour its unread secret. The blackened ashes dropped into the candle holder. "Now it is only you who knows the secret," smiled John Thurloe. "After all, you would not like me to bump you on the head and run off and sell the treasure to the highest bidder, would you now!" he suggested with a laugh.

Matthew also laughed at this ridiculous image which started him coughing once again. The two men carried on with their conversation remembering the days they shared together at the Inns of Court and the ale they had quaffed in their youth. John told Matthew about the illness raging in London and also mentioned how Oliver Cromwell's personal physician had developed a cure against most illnesses, including the plague and proceeded to tell him how Oliver Cromwell had personally taken pains to give John a small bottle of this tincture. John reached inside his tunic and produced the small medicine bottle. He placed drops of the miracle cure into Matthew's bedside water and lifted his head from the pillow and helped his friend to drink deeply of the draught.

"There, I'll let you rest in peace. You will feel better in the morning Matthew, trust me, and now you must get some sleep."

"John," said Matthew, "I have met many people in my life, but I am pleased I can count upon you as my friend. You have my trust in all things."

"Rest now, my dear friend," said Thurloe as he moved away from Matthew's bedside and left the room and the now empty cup. Silently he closed the door behind him, and stood alone outside of his long-standing friend's room, his back to the door, and then he composed him-self and took a deep breath before walking to his own room.

Matthew Hopkins, Witchfinder General died quietly and alone during the night.

Few were surprised, certainly not John Thurloe or Oliver Cromwell.

After all, everyone knew he had been poorly for quite a while. There was little fuss made, his laying out was plain, simple and quick and his body was taken to St Mary's Church at Mistley Heath where it was interred in the grave yard by the new Rector, John Witham. The Rector was secretly over joyed that one of his first deeds in his new parish was to inter the famous Matthew Hopkins and give praise for his soul. Secretly he hoped this may even bring the curious to his small country church. Alms were always welcome to aid the poor of the parish. It was just a few short hours from Matthew's passing to the new incumbent saying a few humble, well-chosen words over the plain unadorned coffin. Only a handful of people were at the graveside and none present recognised the stranger from London, they certainly did not know his name. Within minutes of the burial, the Rector had returned to the church and recorded in the parish register "Mathew Hopkins sone of Mr James Hopkins Minister of Wenham was buryed at Mistley, August 12th 1647"

A plain and simple ending to a short but full and some might even argue infamous life.

While the ink was drying in the parish registry John Thurloe had left the village churchyard and was spurring his horse back along the hot, dusty roads to London.

Oliver Cromwell and John Thurloe knew now the lost Crown Jewels of King John would never be discovered. At their meeting with Matthew Hopkins both men had immediately grasped the fact that once they were revealed to the world, they would act as a rallying point for Royalist forces, both abroad and at home. Too many people, religions and countries wanted a stake in England. After all, the thought of possessing the Crown of Saint Edward the Confessor would be enough to galvanise any true Royalist to war. There had already been too many deaths, too many Kings, too many Crowns, too many plots. Cromwell and Thurloe had no intention of executing one King, removing his crown and replacing it with another. They both knew they could never trust Matthew Hopkins not to reveal his secret. It was a secret which must die, along with the man.

The treasure had lain in dark silence for hundreds of years and now, once again, all trace of it had disappeared, and this time not even Oliver Cromwell or John Thurloe knew where Matthew had hidden it. Its secrecy was absolute. Both men prayed it would never be found. Its future obscurity should prevail.

There was a nation to unite, a King to destroy, peace to be made and a country to be rebuilt.

These were far nobler causes than igniting petty squabbles over mere Royalist baubles.

Dramatis Personae

Matthew Hopkins

Matthew was the fourth of six children, the son of James Hopkins, a puritan clergyman from Great Wenham in Suffolk. His date of birth is unknown but most historians agree it to have been about 1619, by the time of his father's death, he would have been a teenager of around 15 years of age. Matthew was brought up in Great Wenham within a fairly well to do and respected family, It can be safely assumed he would have considerable knowledge of the district and would be familiar with the tales, legends and traditions of witchcraft.

Little is known of the detail of his early education as no records of his school attendance have been found. It is more than probable he was educated by his father. It is also safe to assume he received a proficient education. People of the status of James Hopkins often employed private tutors in areas of education where children such as Matthew may have needed a little help. It is known he could read and write both English and Latin and that he had a working knowledge of both maritime law and insurance. Matthew had in fact worked as a clerk for a ship owner in the village of Mistley where he later owned and Inn, (called the Thorn Inn.) This indicated his ability to learn, and is obviously borne out by his understanding of the ins and outs of the Witchcraft Act and other relevant laws on the statute during this period, laws with which he flew very close to the wind in their interpretation. His later education was directed by his mother. This is indicated in his father's will.

It is not outside the realms of probability that Matthew may have been sent abroad to relatives and received some education overseas. This may well have helped him with his chances of being articled, especially if he had picked up a working knowledge of Flemish or French.

Matthew is next heard of in Ipswich and from there he moved to Manningtree. A reference is made to him being, "*A lawyer of but little note.*" His signature also appears on a legal document dated 1641.

As indicated in his father's will, it would seem likely that Matthew would come into his inheritance on his 22nd birthday which would have been around 1641. It is around this time he bought the "Thorn Inn" at Mistley. It is from here he led his crusade against witchcraft. In '*The Tendring Witchcraft Revelations*' (the title of an unpublished manuscript by C. S. Perryman dated 1725,) It states he "*set himselfe up at Mistley Thorn, from which place he embraced for his conspiracies and to which cam his manie informers againste the Witches and at the Thorn alsoe there cam such celebrated personnes as the Number One Argus, John Thurlowe and William Lilly, the astrological prophet and almanacker*".

From this we can see how Hopkins used the Thorn Inn as the base from which to increase his influence among the countries celebrated and political elite. It is believed his family home was in nearby Manningtree.

Since 1642, civil war had been raging throughout the country and the county of Essex was a staunch supporter of the Roundhead or Parliamentarian cause. Hopkins, like other ruthless men before him, was able to manipulate the prevailing mood of uncertainty, fear, tension and anxiety to turn public opinion to his own advantage. As the Civil War raged, the need to exchange information was perhaps what brought such a diverse group of people together at the Thorn Inn. Hopkins it seems was ideally located and able to exploit and gain through these meetings and contacts, the approbation and support he needed for the witch-hunts which followed.

His first real taste of witch hunting seems to have started in 1645 when he was appointed assistant to John Stearne. What happens next is well documented. His short lived witch hunting career lasted only about two years, but a deadly and tragic two years which still fascinates people, even now.

The eventual fate of Hopkins remains a mystery. There have been various theories as to how he died. The most likely cause of death was given by John Stearne who became his faithful assistant, in a role reversal, who related in his own book "*A Confirmation and Discovery of Witch-craft*" - (London 1648), that he passed away, "*peacefully, after a long sicknesse of a Consumption*". Records show he died in the village of Mistley, presumable at the Thorn Inn, where according to the "Church Registers," he was buried on the 12th August 1647.

Indeed the discovery of factual evidence about his demise was not reported until nearly two centuries after his death, when it appeared in Notes @ Queries, 1st series, vol. 10, p.283, 7th Oct 1854, of which the entry reads:

"*Matthew Hopkins, son of Mr James Hopkins, Minister of Wenham, was buried at Mistley, August 12th, 1647*".

I have visited the site of the old church where he was interred and little remains of the structure, just small pieces of wall and scattered stones and bricks. It seemed strangely disconcerting to be strolling around the site on a summer afternoon, knowing at some stage I was within feet of his final resting place.

Matthew died at the age of 27.

John Stearne

John Stearne (c. 1610-1670) was a staunch puritan, a family man and land owner from Lawshall near Bury St Edmunds. He was a witch-hunter active during the end of the English Civil War period. John Stearne was commissioned by the local magistrates to 'question' a suspected witch, Elizabeth Clarke held in Colchester in March 1645. He employed Matthew Hopkins as his assistant after meeting him in Manningtree. This one original accusation led to a catastrophe for the local female population as many more were accused after confessions were extracted from Elizabeth Clarke. A trial was held in Chelmsford in July 1645 for 33 people accused of witchcraft and sorcery. Of these 4 had died in prison prior to the trial and 15 were subsequently hanged along with the original defendant, Elizabeth Clarke. Four were taken back to Manningtree, home of Matthew Hopkins, and hanged on the village green. Nine who had been convicted of conjuring spirits were reprieved.

Questioning was carried out with the assistance of female searchers. The task of these women was to physically examine the suspect for signs: the devil's marks. These could be warts, moles or bits of extra skin which were declared to be 'teats' to give suckle to imps and familiars. The searchers would sometimes also prick the marks to see if the witch felt pain. The 'witch' would be interrogated and 'watched' for three days and nights, going without sleep, food or water

Stearne was known at various times as the "witch-hunter" and the "witch pricker". Stearne was 10 years older than Hopkins.

Within a year of the death of Matthew Hopkins, John Stearne and his female assistant, the widow Mary Phillips had retired. It was during this period he wrote, "A Confirmation and Discovery of Witchcraft."

John Stearne died peacefully in 1670 at the age of 60. He had retired from his deadly profession over twenty years previously.

<u>Miles Corbett</u>

Miles was born in 1595, the second son of Sir John Corbet, a Norfolk baronet; his education was at Christ's College, Cambridge, and Lincoln's Inn. He was elected MP for Great Yarmouth in the Parliament of 1628, and in the Short and Long Parliaments of 1640. Corbet was active on many parliamentary committees and played a leading role in the organization of the formidable Eastern Association army during the First Civil War.

Corbet was appointed to the High Court of Justice for the trial of King Charles in 1649. He attended only one session of the trial, but signed the King's death warrant. His signature is the last of the 59 names which appear on the warrant. He would later be hunted down as a Regicide.

In October 1650, he was appointed one of the Commonwealth's four civil commissioners in Ireland, and in 1655 he became Chief Baron of the Exchequer in Ireland. Corbet escaped to the Netherlands at the Restoration but was betrayed by the English ambassador Sir George Downing and returned to England for execution.

Hopkins and Corbet worked together on several witch trials. Miles was chairman of the much feared Committee of Examinations. Miles Corbet was the Recorder at King's Lynn during the witch trials described in the book.

He was hanged, drawn and quartered along with John Barkstead and John Okey at Tyburn on 19 April 1662.

He died at the age of 67.

<u>The Kings Lynn Witch Trial</u>

MATTHEW AND THE KILDERKIN

The witch trial featured in the book took place as described. The nine were accused after the finger of suspicion was pointed their way. A panel of midwives and *"honest matrons"* had discovered suspicious marks on their bodies. Hopkins was awarded the sum of £15 for his handling of the case. This was about the amount which the drummer who escorted the men through the town on their arrival could hope to earn in sixteen months. It must be remembered Hopkins was invited to the town to gather and record proof against those people who had already been charged by the townsfolk.

The charge against the accused, most of whom were widows was of, *"felonious witchcraft and feloniously consulting and covenanting with an evil spirit."* All the accused pleaded not guilty to the charges levied against them. The trial was held with various civic Aldermen, Justices and keepers of the gaol in attendance.

Matthew Hopkins himself gave evidence against Thomas Dempster in whose body search he had participated along with the personal searches of the widows Taylor and Browne. Most of the other witnesses who gave evidence were the watchers and searchers. The jury only found two people to be guilty. This was not the outcome Hopkins or his fellow accusers had intended. Most people thought the verdicts to be an unexpected and lenient surprise. It had been anticipated most of the accused would hang. The sentence was carried out in the Tuesday market place at Kings Lynn.

Hopkins was paid another £2 for giving evidence and left the town shortly afterwards. Some say he was embarrassed by the poor result. The verdicts were as follows:

Grace Wright, a widow, was convicted to be hanged.
Katherine Banks, a widow, was acquitted.

Emma Godfrey, a widow, was acquitted.

Cecily Taylor, a widow, was acquitted

Lydia Browne, a widow, was judged to be "*non compos mentis*" and therefore deemed not fit enough to be tried. She was released.

Dorothy Griffin was acquitted

Thomasine Parker was acquitted

Dorothy Lee was found guilty and sentenced to be hanged.

Thomas Dempster was a local labourer. He was also acquitted.

<u>James Hopkins</u>

Hopkins senior was a Church of England clergyman. The '*Alumni Cantabrigienses, Pt. 1, vol. Ii, 1922, p. 405, Venn*' shows James Hopkins was Vicar at St John's, Great Wenham in Suffolk from 1612, and he died there in 1634. However, the Great Wenham parish records are incomplete for the period he was incumbent, and its earliest burial records begin in 1665, so his death is not recorded. What has been found is the Will of one of his parishioners: Daniel Wyles of Great Wenham dated 1619, which by association gives us a little insight into the man and his family. In his Will, Wyles made a bequest to:

> "*James Hopkins, preacher of the word of God at Great Wenham and to his wife*", leaving "*6s. 8d each to their children, James, Thomas and John when able to read a chapter in the New Testament, to buy a Bible*".

From this we can speculate James Hopkins and his wife were well liked and respected in the community, and had a young family of three boys not yet able or old enough to read the bible. James had six children and as Matthew is not mentioned in this Will, we can surmise he may not yet have been born. We can also speculate that as the boys had been named after Apostles and Saints that Matthew may have followed soon after, making his birth date somewhere around or after 1619.

Just before his death, James Hopkins wrote and left his own Will, which was written, sealed and witnessed on Christmas day in 1634.

The last Will and Testament of James Hopkins.

I, James Hopkins, of Wenham Magna in the County of Suffolk, Clerke, being weake in body but of a perfect & good disposeing mynd & memorye, I thanke God, doe Make my laste Will & Testament in Manner ffollowinge. I first of all doe freely surrender My soule into the hands of Allmighty God, trusting that (I) shalbe receved to Mercy onely through the Righteousness & Merritts of the Lorde Jesus Christ my Saviour & I yeald my body to the Earth to be buried accordinge & Where my Executrix shall thinke Moste Meete; & Wheereas I am seised to Mee & My heires of Certayne lands & tenements in fframlingham at the Castle in the County aforesayde I give & bequeath all My Sayde Lands, & Tenements, unto Marie My welbeloved Wife & her heires payeing and dischargeing the porcions ensueing bequeathed to my Children; that is to say payinge unto eache of my sixe Children severally when & so soone as they or eyther off them shall accomplishe the age of Two and twenty yeares the somme off One hundred Markes of Currant Money of England. Never the lesse as touchinge My sonne Thomas My Mynde & Will is that my Executrix shall as soone as she can finde opportunitie send him over the seaes to such our frinds in Newe England as she shall thinke fitt & that he shall theire abyde until hee shall accomplishe the sayd age of two and twenty yeeres & so soone as he shall have accomplished the sayd age, then I will that my Executrix shall paye him the sayd somme of one hundred Marks, deductinge therefromme the Chardge which shee shall disburse in sendinge him over the seaes, by the direction of My sayd Wife; & shall (he?) not alsoe stay there until he shall accomplishe the age aforesaid, then I will that he shall not have any benefit of this My said will Nor of the sayd One hundred Marks formerly bequeathed To him & furthermore if any of my sayd Children shall departe the(i)re present life before they severally shall accomplish theire ages of two and twenty yeeres as aforesayde then the porcion of such child or children soe dyeinge shalbe Equally devided betweene the surviveors of them at there severall ages aforesayde, Item I will that my Executrix shall paye unto My sistar Lane at Elye forty shillings yeerely duringe her life, & unto Anne Lane my servant twenty nobles. Item I give to my eldest James all my bookes, & all the Reste of my Goodes & Chattles I give them to Marie my lovinge Wife whom I doe make My sole Executrix for My last Will requireinge her to take advise of true Worthy frinds Mr John Gurden of Wenham aforesaid, & Mr Natthaniell Bacon & prayeinge them to give there beste furtherance and advice unto her in all diffculte matters, that doe or Maye concerne the Executing thereof. Lastlye I leave My children to the direction & government of my wife Requireinge them to yeeld unto her all dutiful respecte as they shall answere yt to God & also Requireinge her to looke to theire educacion according to her beste skill that they may be brought up in the feare of God & in such honest callinge as shall best suite with their disposiciones & estates; & I doe declare this to be My last Will and Testament; hereby Revokeinge & adnullinge all former Wills or Wrightings in the Nature of Wills, or wrightings tendinge thereunto & in witness hereof I doe here adioyne My hand & seale this twentye five daye of December in the yeere of our Lorde God One thousand six hundred thyrte & fower in the presence of John Gurdon Roger London.

While this Will again makes no mention to Matthew by name, it does lead us to further insights and speculation about his early life.

John Hopkins

In September 1645, John Hopkins of Wenham (almost certainly Matthew's older brother) is described in parish records as being Presbyterian and was the appointed 'Minister of South Fambridge' in Essex. There is also an additional note from a year later in June 1646, stating there had been complaints that John Hopkins had neglected his work and been replaced.

Again the parish records for both North and South Fambridge are incomplete but one reference indicates: *"a list of eight subscribers to brief for French Protestants"*. The area of Fambridge during this time had strong Puritan associations with many links to the French Huguenots. After the St Bartholomew's day Massacre in France 1572, an estimated 40,000 Huguenot refugees left France for England, and many settled in this area of East Anglia. Marie Hopkins, Matthew's mother, is thought to have come from

Huguenot stock and provided the Puritan influence in the Hopkins family.

John Thurloe

John Thurloe was born in 1616, the son of Thomas Thurloe, the rector of Abbess Roding in Essex. Being about the same age as Hopkins, he had studied law as a young man through which profession they may have made initial contact. At the time of their meetings in the Thorn Inn, and as his eventual title of '*Number One Argus*' would indicate, he was well on the road to becoming Cromwell's 'Chief of the Secret Service.' In 1645, Thurloe was appointed one of the Secretaries to the Commissioners of Parliament at the Treaty of Uxbridge, and thus may well have become Hopkins' link to other sources of Government in London. John was also admitted to Lincolns Inn around this time. He was twice married and died at his legal chambers at Lincoln Inns in 1668 at the age of 52.

In 1653 Thurloe's career as an official spymaster included being made Post-Master General, where he had the power to intercept any letters which he thought may be detrimental to the stability of the Protectorate. He also had the power to suppress most Newsbooks of the period, except for Mercurius Politicus and The Public Intelligencer, both of which were Government controlled. Thurloe realised the importance of controlling the media even then. His agents infiltrated Charles II's court-in-exile and he employed the mathematician and cryptographer John Wallis to break Royalist ciphers. John Thurloe grew a reputation for apparently always being one step ahead of his enemies. He was the "M" of his time. He was among those who urged Cromwell to accept the Crown in 1657. Thurloe admired Cromwell as a ruler and was a personal friend of Oliver Cromwell.

John Thurloe was secretive to the end and his papers are of huge importance to historians of the Protectorate period. They were eventually found hidden behind a false ceiling in his former chambers at Lincoln's Inn during the reign of William III. No mention was made of a plot to kill Matthew Hopkins. His private collection was eventually presented to the Bodleian Library at Oxford.

William Lilly

William Lilly was born on May-day in 1602 and by the time of the Thorn Inn meetings with Matthew Hopkins had become one the country's leading and most influential astrologers. He had contacts and friends on both sides of the political 'civil war' divide, as well as with prominent politicians and members of the countries aristocracy. Hopkins undoubtedly consulted with Lilly: *"on various matters relating to shippes and cargoes as well as some darker aspects of the Signes of the Times appertayning to witchcraft amonge other things"*.

William Lilly died in 1681 at the age of 79.

It is generally regarded that Lilly's most comprehensive book was entitled *Christian Astrology*. It was published in 1647, the year of Hopkins' death. It remains popular even today and has never gone totally out-of-print, it is so large it came in three separate volumes in modern times, and is considered one of the classic texts for the study of traditional astrology from the Middle-Ages. Its popularity was mainly due to the fact it was the first such book to be written in English rather than Latin.

About the Author

Pete lives in Cornwall, England and loves old English folk traditions and customs, such as Wassailing and following the Padstow 'obby 'oss on May Day. He has also dressed up and participated in period re-enactments for well over forty years. The English Civil War is still his preferred period of history. Here Pete is shown at a recent battle re-enactment, proving that even sixty year olds can still carry a pike and fight on the field of War. Albeit in the cause of charity!

Having had three careers, working in silk screen printing within the pharmaceutical industry, technical theatre involved with lighting and lighting design and finally his own shop selling European style board games and puzzles. Pete is now filling his time writing and pottering around on film sets as an "extra". He is happily married and seems to have also picked up a menagerie of squirrels, birds and ducks, which daily visit his Cornish cottage garden.

Authors Notes;

I spent many happy hours around the towns of Manningtree and Kings Lynn, researching the background for the book and discovered some beautiful places whilst there. The village of Mistley Heath contains the now ruined church, where the body of Matthew Hopkins was laid to rest. It is nestled down a quiet lane behind a small red brick wall and is full of atmosphere. When I visited, there were just some contented sheep to keep me company. This location will be re-visited in more detail in the fourth book in the "Trust" series, entitled, "Orlando's Quest."

The church where Matthew grew up in the village of Great Wenham will also be visited in more detail in the third book in the series, "Doyle and Wells."

This is the second in a series of four books entitled, "The Trust," which follows the trail of a treasure unearthed, lost and hidden through different time periods.

The first is entitled: "The Spy, The Dwarf and the Mongol"

This is a medieval tale of monarchs, codes, myth and murder, explaining one of the greatest mysteries of the age. Join this epic journey which takes you from the camp of Genghis Kahn through the heart of the Templars, to the very King of England! An original story which might just make you question what you think you know about history.

You may download the first 25% of the book free courtesy of the Author.

www.smashwords.com/books/view/496590[1]

Available formats: epub, mobi (kindle), pdf, rtf, lrf, pdb, txt, and html

All the books in the "Trust" series will be available soon on Smashwords.

---

1. https://www.smashwords.com/books/view/496590

Author's Acknowledgements

The author would like to thank everyone who has freely given me their time to beta read various drafts over the last few years and have been generous enough to give me their feedback. You know who you are guys.

A special "thank you" goes to my old friend Ian Scott for his help with the final corrections and edit.

Thanks must also go to; my friends in the Sealed Knot, who have given me a practical understanding since the early 1970's on everything Civil War related. This ranges from period etiquette to all things military and from the true value of friendship to learning how to still stand erect in a beer tent after imbibing far too many pints of English ale.

I am especially indebted to Malcolm Gaskill whose book "Witchfinders ~ A Seventeenth-Century English Tragedy" proved to be an endless source of enlightenment and insight into the world surrounding the turmoil of the East Anglian witch-hunts of the mid 1640's. This is a fabulous book and one which is well worth owning.

Appreciation and thanks for a great looking cover goes to Diversepixel, whose work can be found at; www.selfpubbookcovers.com/[1]

On a more serious note, we should all remember the dreadful times and experiences endured by all the victims, their friends and families who suffered endless torments at the hands of the people who accused and prosecuted the crime of witchcraft. Grace Wright, Katherine Banks, Emma Godfrey, Cecily Taylor, Lydia Browne, Dorothy Griffin, Thomasine Parker, Dorothy and Thomas Dempster. These were real people from the Kings Lynn area who were among thousands who were hunted down, persecuted and prosecuted across Europe and fell under the prey of those enveloped with a Godly zeal and fervour. This book will help to keep them in our collective memory.

Finally, this book is dedicated to Helen, my wonderful ex-wife, for all her support, patience and inspiration and to our cats Boot, who seemed to always want fuss while helping me with my typing and of course Puss, who loved lying in the sun, sleeping and eating. We wish you were both with us now.

Special thanks goes to Gabrielle O'Connor my beautiful partner for her encouragement, help and support in getting this book into print and in supporting me with all my other madcap adventures, schemes and ideas.

I am also proud to have four wonderfully gifted and unique step daughter, Ciara, Charlotte, Lucy and Leah who always light up my life with their smiles and antics.

---

1. http://www.selfpubbookcovers.com/

"The Trust"

This is the second in a series of four books entitled, "The Trust," which follows the trail of a treasure unearthed, lost and hidden through different time periods.

The first book is called "The Spy, The Dwarf and the Mongol." This is a medieval tale of monarchs, codes, myth and murder, explaining one of the greatest mysteries of the age. Join this epic journey which takes you from the camp of Genghis Kahn through the heart of the Templars, to the very King of England! This chapter in time ended with an act of audacity which had far reaching consequences. Indeed it just might make you question what you thought you knew about history.

The third is entitled, "Doyle and Wells." The time frame is the 1890's. It features Sir Arthur Conan Doyle and H G Wells in a Victorian world of séances, mystery and investigation. Sir Arthur Conan Doyle is contacted through the spirit world by a woman seeking peace and retribution. This leads Doyle and his young friend Wells on a treasure hunt. Along the way they encounter Bram Stoker, Sir Henry Irving, The Golden Dawn, and Dr Joseph Bell, his mentor and friend on whom he based the character of Sherlock Holmes. To misquote Doyle, "The game's afoot!"

The final book is called, "Orlando's Quest." It has a contemporary setting and features, Orlando Porthtowan, an old Cornish raconteur and collector of ephemera who buys several personal letters written by the long dead Sir Arthur Conan Doyle. These lead Orlando to discovering an enigma with diverse clues hidden safely within a Sherlock Holmes story. A secret treasure map hidden in plain view for over a hundred years! He knows he may have stumbled upon something of great interest, but will he be able to unravel the riddle with the help of his two young friends the Easterbrook's? Will they, or indeed you, solve the mystery in the clues left by Doyle from beyond the grave?

Each book in "The Trust" series is a stand-alone novel and you do not have to have read the others in order, but the continuity will enhance your enjoyment.

Wassail!

Also by Pete Minall

The Spy, The Dwarf & The Mongol
Matthew and the Kilderkin
Doyle and Wells
Orlando's Quest

Watch for more at peteminall.wix.com/the-trust.

Milton Keynes UK
Ingram Content Group UK Ltd.
UKHW021536230924
448709UK00003B/18